LOVE IS THE LAW

THAT OLD BLACK MAGIC: HEART'S DESIRED MATE

MELISSA SNARK

LOVE IS THE LAW

WORLD: THAT OLD BLACK MAGIC

SERIES: HEART'S DESIRED MATE

ISBN-13: 978-1-942193-27-2 (ebook)

ISBN-13: 978-1-942193-28-9 (paperback)

Cover design by Monica La Porta

Contact Information:

Email: admin@nordiclightspress.com

Nordic Lights Press

P.O. Box 1347

Pleasanton, CA 94566

Published in the United States of America.

ACKNOWLEDGMENTS

That Old Black Magic has been a wonderful and rewarding adventure in creating a shared world. It couldn't have happened without the support and cooperation of some fantastic authors. My thanks go to Ann Gimpel, Julia Lake Mills, Monica La Porta, J.C. McKenzie, Ava Michaels, Vonnie Davis, and T.F. Walsh. Thank you to my editors, Shay VanZwoll of EV Proofreading, and Ekatarina Sayanova of Red Quill Editing. Thank you to Tammy Payne of Book Nook Nuts Proofreading. Special thanks to my cover designer, Monica La Porta.

Hotshot LA lawyer Chase Baron doesn't know whether to kiss or throttle his best friend's little sister. She's a spoiled, unpredictable brat, and she drives this alpha wolf shifter howling mad. The last thing he wants is a chaotic witch disrupting his orderly life. When magic frees him of all his inhibitions, his wolf claims his one true mate. Once the claiming is over, however, he's left mired in resentment over his lover's manipulation.

Arabia Jensen doesn't mean to cause trouble. It's her natural-born talent as a raven shifter. She casts a Heart's Desire spell intended to capture the attention of a certain stubborn werewolf. But after the magic takes hold, she's the one who loses control.

Arabia finds more than just her hands full with a big bad wolf who's horny and lookin' for love.

Once the pandemonium fades, Arabia's antics land her in prison. Chase is the only attorney willing to take her case, but even he thinks she's guilty. What's a woman to do when the man she loves believes she's committed crimes of the heart?

CHAPTER 1

JAILBIRD BLUES

December 5th...

It'd been a shitty month.

The scratchy prison uniform itched—orange was her *worst* color—and the man Arabia Jensen loved wanted to kill her. "No," she said flatly. "It ain't happening."

"No?" Chase Baron asked as though he hadn't heard her correctly. But he had; she knew he had because he was fully engaged. She could tell from the intensity of his gaze and the way he wrung his hands, probably imagining them wrapped around her neck, and ground his teeth in aggravation. The alpha of the Baron Pack had his wolf in his eyes: fully dilated pupils framed by gold irises that eclipsed the whites.

"No." Arabia cocked her head, a habitual gesture derived from her raven-shifter nature. Ravens were quick, cunning tricksters, and she got her mischievous tendencies from her avian aspect. These landed her in trouble often, but never anything she couldn't charm or think her way out of.

Well, up until now anyway. This time, her boldness and really bad luck had landed Arabia in the Stillwater Correctional Facility.

"No." Chase sat straighter, and the molded plastic chair creaked beneath his muscular bulk. The penitentiary conference room had cheap furniture and a white tile floor, and it offered minimal privacy. From the next room, a female guard watched the prisoner and her attorney through a reinforced glass window; supposedly, the woman couldn't eavesdrop on them.

"No, what? You refuse to sign?" Chase exhaled through flared nostrils. He radiated aggression under pressure, a sexy-as-hell volcano on the verge of eruption. The six-feet-five, two hundred pounds of pure muscle werewolf exuded a dangerous aura wholly at odds with his buttoned-down appearance. People often accused ravenborn of shenanigans and chicanery. But the alpha wolf's civilized facade qualified as outright deceit, starting with his conservative black suit and tie. His neatly trimmed mustache and beard accentuated his already devilishly handsome charisma. The gold hoop in his earlobe hinted at the rebellious streak Chase liked to suppress and Arabia wished he'd unleash far more often.

"That's right. I can't sign this." Arabia curled her lower lip and held her hand over the legal document —a thick sheaf of papers bound with an alligator clip —on the table. She stabbed at it with her finger. In her distaste, she couldn't stand to touch it, so she settled for pointing.

"You're refusing to sign," Chase said again.

"That's what I said. Your hearing must be failing. Should I talk louder?" Arabia snapped. The words flew from her lips. She regretted the smartass remark the second she said it. Her fingers twitched, and she crushed the fidgety reflex to cover her mouth. *Too late!* She supposed it'd be the ultimate irony if the guards meant to confine her wound up having to come to her rescue.

The air crackled.

"My hearing is fine. I just don't like what you're saying." A slight flush crept up Chase's neck and across his face, and his smooth skin rippled in waves raised over iron-hard bands of sinew.

He huffed and he puffed, every menacing inch the big, bad wolf of her fantasies. He placed his palms flat and dug his fingernails into the chipped tabletop. If his formidable self-control slipped another millimeter, he could reduce the plywood to splinters... the brick walls to rubble...

Delightful shivers coursed down Arabia's spine. She knew it was wrong, but she fucking *loved* punching Chase's buttons. Pushing him right to the edge. If she couldn't bask in the heat of his passion, she'd settle for the glare of brooding anger. Before she thought it through, she retorted, "Well, that's just too damn bad."

"Damn it, Arabia! Stop being so damn contrary." With a roar, Chase shot to his feet and smashed his fists down on the table. It shattered into pieces. His lost temper set land speed records: from polished poise to nail-spitting mad in three seconds flat.

Arabia leapt off her chair and would've taken flight except for the enchanted bracelets she wore on her wrists, which prevented shape changing. Excitement poured through her along with the burn of adrenaline in her muscles. At the same time, the narrow confines of the room aggravated her claustrophobia.

"I'm not being contrary. I can explain if you'd just

listen." Arabia didn't believe Chase would hurt her, but she retreated to the edge of the room to be safe. She'd never seen Chase so mad, and that was saying a lot. The raven-shifter had pretty much spent her entire life as far back as she could remember aggravating Chase. At times, she secretly suspected her birth had somehow pissed the then eight-year-old Chase off. Not to be immodest, but she considered herself the world's leading authority on provoking the man.

"Alpha Baron, stand down!" The guard's command came across the static-ridden intercom. It counted as evidence of Chase's stature that the woman didn't immediately rush in with her Taser charged. Arabia had been a prisoner long enough to have witnessed multiple confrontations. The prison staff loved to practice baton diplomacy.

Chase halted mid-stride. A growl reverberated in his throat, and he waged an inner struggle, which played out on his face and across his body. A ferocious grimace. The combative set of his shoulders. Man versus beast, ever at primordial odds.

Arabia watched the conflict with avid fascination. She stole a quick glance through the window. The female guard stared at Chase as though he was an all-course Las Vegas buffet. A jealous twinge bit Arabia. She saw green. The guard might as well have had a dribble of drool running down her chin

Bitch needed a bib.

"I'm standing down," Chase said in an even tone. He raised his hands, signaling his surrender. Predictably, the alpha's innate dislike of obedience kicked in. In less than a second, he turned the gesture into an excuse to tighten the knot on his tie.

"Thank you. Please resume your seats. I do have to warn you. Your session with your client will be over if this happens again," the guard said, sounding comically relieved and deferential at once.

Arabia puckered her mouth. What a little toady!

"Understood." Chase frowned at the ruined table. "I'll pay for the damages, of course. Have the bill sent to my law firm."

"Yes, sir." The intercom clicked off.

"Yes, sir. No, sir. Anything for *you*, sir," Arabia mocked with a sneer.

Chase leaned over and fished the plea bargain document out of the wreckage of the ruined table. He caught the back of his chair and set it upright, facing the one Arabia had vacated. He leveled an unwavering stare and toed her chair toward her. "Sit."

"*Oh, yes sir.*" She flipped her straight, black

Cleopatra hair *and* her middle finger. With an odious cough, she pantomimed gagging behind her fist.

Chase chuckled, low and soft. It flowed over her like warm water. Arabia blinked and bubbled at the unexpected expression. He entreated in a velvet voice, "Please."

Without thinking, Arabia plunked down. In the aftermath, she fumed. Damn the man and his alpha's trick—using vocal magic to make her obey. In a querulous whine, she complained, "That's cheating."

"Whatever it takes to get the job done." He flashed a shameless smile and assumed the seat opposite her.

"That sounds distinctly at odds with your law and order philosophy." She ran her hand through her hair, trying to soothe her restive anxiety. When she encountered limp dryness, it served to agitate her further. Closer inspection revealed a ton of split ends.

"Law and order is more deeply rooted in pragmatism than you'd think."

She shrugged. "If you say so. I wouldn't know."

He heaved a heavy sigh and pressed his lips together. The atmosphere grew strained. After a pause, he changed the topic. "I'm worried about you, Arabia. You don't look good."

She flinched from his quiet intimacy. The demonstration of concern hurt far worse than any angry outburst he might've lashed out with. And that he'd noticed her state of disrepair added insult to injury. Oh, wounded vanity!

The last month in lockup had ruined her appearance. Her teal highlights had faded, and her unshaven legs looked like they belonged to Lady Bigfoot. Inmates weren't allowed hair dye or razors... or, apparently, to look good. Her hands were chaffed and raw from being assigned to dishwashing detail, and the harsh detergent used in the prison laundry had given her patchy rashes over her entire body. Another month in this place and she'd look like a gorilla.

She *needed* out.

Arabia faced trial on multiple counts of felonious misuse of magic. At the arraignment hearing, the judge had declared, "The court deems Arabia Jensen of the Silverwind Conspiracy to be too much of a flight risk. Bail is denied." Adding insult to injury, that humorless magistrate had pronounced the pun without even cracking a smile.

Arabia hadn't been amused. *Flight risk, my tail feathers! Ffffffffffff.*

"Yeah, I know I look like crap. Thanks for the reminder!" Arabia bristled in defensive reflex.

A thunderous scowl crossed his face. "That's not what I meant."

"I know. I'm sorry. I shouldn't have snapped at you." Arabia gulped down a breath and strove to get her emotions under control. Unshed tears stung her eyes, and her throat ached.

Habitually, she fidgeted because she wasn't able to stay still. Her fingers found and latched onto the ornate solid gold bead worn at the base of a small braid beneath her ear. It was the only piece of jewelry she had left, and she'd only managed to hold onto it because she kept it hidden under her hair. The authorities had confiscated the rest of her pretty, sparkly trinkets, which all ravenborn adored. They'd taken something far more precious than comfort and physical luxuries. Those bastards had stolen her freedom. The enchanted bracelets prevented her from being able to shape shift. Without wings, she couldn't fly.

The loss of flight wounded her soul.

"Let's take this again from the top. This is the plea bargain I negotiated with the DA. Signing it will secure your immediate release. It's a good deal. You should take it. As your attorney, I'm advising you to take it. So why won't you sign it?" He jostled the document so the pages rustled, adding emphasis to his point.

"It's not that I won't sign it. I *can't* sign it." She bit her chafed lips and hunched over in abject misery. A stubborn thread of pride kept her from wrapping her arms around herself in a self-hug. She couldn't stand to be so pathetic in front of Chase. His opinion mattered to her more than she cared to admit.

Chase's expression softened with what might've been sympathy, but it proved elusive, that proverbial mirage on the horizon. His face hardened, set into a stoic mask. His eyes remained wolf gold, having never reverted to human. "We're going in circles. For the moment, let's set aside whether you'll sign it. Tell me, *why* you think you can't."

Arabia perked up. Ah ha! Maybe Chase was ready to finally *listen* to what she had to say. She snatched the document from his hands and flipped through the pages until she located the pertinent one —the reason behind her adamant refusal to put her John Hancock on the signature line.

Determined to make her point, she tapped her fingertip over the point of contention. Her nails were ragged from constant chewing, a bad habit, but it was how she dealt with the stress of confinement. "It says I'm guilty."

Chase cast a cursory glance over the indicated line. His breath hissed when he exhaled. Then, in the ultimate insult possible, he addressed her as though she was child. "That is indeed what it says. That's how a plea bargain works. In exchange for your admission and a hefty fine, which *I'm* paying, the charges will be dropped. You'll be released with time served."

"And you don't have a problem with this?" Arabia crossed her arms over her breasts, feeling completely exposed and vulnerable. How could Chase not see how this was utterly wrong? In every way imaginable.

"No, why would I? You *are* guilty." Chase's tone struck a harsh note, like a hammer on smelted steel. There it was again: bitter condemnation. He blamed her for what had happened. Oh, he tried to hide it, and he usually succeeded. Every now and then, however, his guard slipped, and she caught a glimpse of the angry accusation he harbored in his heart.

"I'm not! And my own attorney shouldn't judge me." Tightness in her throat made it difficult to breathe. Arabia unfolded her arms and clenched her fists.

Her lover shouldn't condemn her.

"I'm not judging you." Chase reached over and plucked the plea bargain from her fingers. Such a control freak. It must've gotten his boxers into a real twist, allowing her to hold onto it as long as she had.

"Yeah, you are." The desire to thwart him provoked her. Impulsively, she summoned a gust of wind using her ravenborn magic. It blasted through the conference area, whipping her hair about her face. The paperwork fluttered like crazy, but the metal clasp kept it from flying away.

"Knock it off. You know magic is an infraction of the rules." Chase employed a tone of command. In the face of her turmoil, the man remained as maddeningly cool and remote as an Arctic iceberg.

Arabia jutted her jaw in stubborn defiance. She disliked being ordered about, but she despised the prohibition against using her natural-born abilities even more. She opened her mouth to tell him off but caught motion in her peripheral vision. The distraction silenced her.

The female prison guard stationed to observe them had edged closer to the entrance to the meeting room. Apparently, Chase could pulverize furniture to his heart's content, but a stiff breeze earned Arabia the threat of reprisal.

"It also says I'm sorry. I'm not sorry." Arabia slouched, folding her hands on her lap. After a brief hesitation, the guard holstered her baton and returned to her post.

"I swear, I never thought I'd hear myself say this to a client," Chase muttered. "*Lie.* It shouldn't be difficult. Deceit is in your nature."

The insult stung but Arabia had too much pride to let the hurt show. Chase didn't understand. Every day of her month-long incarceration had tested her resolve and worn down her reserves. She endured the humiliation and hardship, however, to prove herself to him. He meant more to her than even her cherished freedom. She would sooner yank her own teeth with rusty pliers than admit to remorse or regret. Renouncing what she'd done meant forsaking him. *Them.* Better to spend the next century rotting in prison than betray her loyalty to the man she considered her soulmate.

The silence stretched.

Chase scowled and leaned toward her. Their gazes locked; tension crackled like caged lightning. "You don't feel the least bit of contrition for what you did?"

"No. Why should I?" It crushed Arabia to confront the harsh condemnation of the only man she'd ever loved. Marshaling all her strength, she squared her shoulders.

"Your love spell started a citywide orgy."

"Oh, orgy!" She huffed. "That's a gross exaggeration!"

The local media had dubbed the incident the Stillwater Orgy Scandal. Arabia scoffed just thinking about it. What an utter joke! As *if* the sleepy community of all-supernatural residents was even big enough to have a scandal. Arabia couldn't begin to understand what the huge fuss was about. The botched love spell had affected a few hundred people, every last one a consenting adult. No one had gotten injured or killed. She hadn't jeopardized the community's secrecy or security. Worst case scenario, the evening might produce a few unplanned pregnancies.

"People were having sex in the streets," Chase grated.

"And how is that a bad thing? For Ceridwen's sake, I helped a whole lot of really repressed people realize their heart's desire. They ought to be thanking me, not locking me up or trying me on bogus charges."

He sputtered. "Your victims had no choice—"

"Oh, it's my victims now, is it? Is that how you perceive yourself, Chase? As my victim?" Arabia asked from beneath lowered lashes. She pressed her clenched fists against her thighs to stop from pummeling him. "Did I force you to rip my clothes off and fuck me against the wall?"

"Arabia." Chase used her name as a warning. A rumble rolled from his throat. His gaze liquefied to molten gold, casting a glow across his face.

Arabia dropped her voice to a sultry murmur and leaned forward. "Were you operating under the influence of magical roofies when you dragged me into the shower and—"

"Stop." He stiffened, and his basal scent spiked with frustration and arousal. Both flavors had characterized his aroma for the last month. There, in his eyes, she saw the truth. He remembered as well as she did, their time together branded into the depths of his memory. The same as hers.

"Tell me again how you weren't an active, willing participant. I dare you," Arabia threw out one final taunt and fell silent. She could've gone on for a while, in explicit detail, about the things he'd done to her. With her. She stopped, however, because of their audience, the prison guard, still watching through the window.

After a moment, Chase recovered his composure. His wolf retreated behind the stoical mask he maintained. When he spoke again, his tone was perfectly normal. "I'm worried about you, Arabia. I can see you're suffering. Confinement isn't good for you."

Arabia cringed. His unexpected sympathy hurt. Her heart ached, and she choked on unwanted tears. "It's been hard. I haven't shifted or flown since they locked me up—"

"I want to help you get out of here." He reached over and covered her hand with his own. His touch sent energy flowing through her. The hairs on the back of her arms stood on end. The unexpectedness of the gesture knocked her even more off kilter. Touching wasn't allowed under prison regulations, and it wasn't like Chase to break rules.

"I want out of here." When she spoke, she blinked. Was that tiny little whisper *her* voice? She blamed it on the tightness in her throat.

Chase exhaled. "Help me get you out of here then. Sign the plea bargain."

"No." Arabia hissed with abrupt insight. Her sorrow gave way to anger. He'd only said those things to manipulate her. Its heat kept her warm and hardened her resolve.

"If you refuse to sign the plea bargain, then you'll have to stand trial. I can't guarantee the outcome. As it stands, you're facing seventeen felony counts of magical coercion of citizens who engaged in sexual intercourse in violation of their free will. Add on possession and felony misuse of a divine essence, and you're facing consecutive life sentences if convicted."

Arabia shuddered. Blood drained from her face, and she was positive she'd turned as white as a ghost. For a minute, her conviction wavered like a sail in a brisk breeze, but then she caught hold of her resolve with the entirety of her will.

"No. No way am I signing this. You can tell them they can take their plea bargain and shove it where the sun doesn't shine."

"And that's your final answer?" Chase ran his hand through his hair, messing up his neat styling. All of a sudden, he seemed exhausted and close to defeat.

Sympathy stabbed at Arabia, but she'd made her choice. She wanted to cry. "Yes, that's my final answer."

Your family is going to be furious." The poor man

must be at his wits' end to resort to playing *that* guilt card.

"I'm sure they will be." Arabia winced just to envision her mother's histrionics when she found out. Her father and sister would be sorrowful and worried. And then there was Reidar, her older brother and Chase's best friend. No matter what, she didn't want to drive a wedge between the two men.

"Good, because you're going to be the one who gets to explain it to them." He shook his head, reinforcing his adamant refusal to the task.

"I'll do it this weekend." She raised her hand in a pledge.

Without fail, her family drove all the way from Los Angeles every weekend to visit her. When she'd first been arrested, Arabia's mother, Evelyn, had threatened to move to Stillwater. It'd taken a whole lot of convincing, including Chase's promise to remain in town until the criminal court case was resolved, to convince Evelyn to stay in LA.

Chase grimaced and shoved the rejected plea bargain into his brief case. "I hope you understand what we're up against, Arabia."

"I do, but I also know that you'll find some way to win." Arabia cocked her head and mustered a sweet, sad smile. She ached to rise and go to him. If only she could place her hand upon his chest and caress the spot over his heart through the fine material of his suit. Maybe then he would feel what she felt and know the truth of her devotion.

He snorted. "We're both fools. You'd better offer up a special sacrifice to your goddess. We're going to need all the help we can get."

"I have faith in you, Chase, even if you don't believe in me."

CHAPTER 2

THE GENTLEMAN WOLF

The lights on the Christmas tree twinkled cheerfully while the antique jukebox pumped out a soulful blues song over the state-of-the-art sound system. The gray-haired man Chase was meeting sat at the mahogany bar, facing the entrance. When Chase paused, Seamus Grayson raised his hand ever so slightly. Chase tipped his chin in acknowledgement and made his way over, navigating the weeknight crowd that qualified as more of a throng than a mob.

The Clover Club, an upscale bar, was across from the courthouse on Main Street in Stillwater, California. The secluded community was situated in the southern Sierra Nevada Mountains, located northeast of the urban jungle that made up the greater Los Angeles area. Its residents were predominantly shifters, although a handful of other supernatural sorts made the city their home. Here magical creatures congregated, free to use their natural abilities without fear of discovery or persecution. Stillwater's remote location and mystical warding shielded its denizens from the outside world ignorant of magic.

Neighboring businesses included Bumble Bee Florist and Baby Bear Day Care. By day, courthouse employees and white-collar professionals from surrounding businesses flocked to the Rise and Grind coffee shop. After dark, the Clover Club served as the favored watering hole. Chase liked the establishment; the faces were familiar even if no one knew his name...

Well, almost no one.

On cue, a man's low voice came from the shadows. "Evening, Baron."

"Evening." Chase returned the greeting by rote. He glanced over, scanning a secluded alcove tucked against the back wall closest to the bar.

Detective Mateo Savage sat alone in the booth. The panther-shifter was hunched over, elbows on the table, nursing a drink. Upon identifying the speaker, Chase's mood dropped to sub-zero for the man in charge of the criminal investigation into

Arabia. To be fair, the lieutenant was only doing his job; however, Chase's wolf harbored a serious grudge. Fortunately, his social obligation ended at salutations.

The men traded stares, and Chase continued to the bar. There, Seamus Grayson acknowledged Chase's arrival with a patient nod, and Laura, the attractive brunette bartender, welcomed Chase with a ready smile.

"Hey there, Chase."

"Evenin', Laura."

The sleek cougar-shifter gave him the usual appraisal. Her appreciative gaze performed a subtle slide across his shoulders and chest. He liked that Laura returned her regard to his face almost immediately. More than once, he'd been tempted to accept the implicit invitation to a one-night stand. His conscience stopped him dead in his tracks. He couldn't take a woman to his bed when all he'd be thinking about was a different lover. It wasn't fair to her or himself.

Damnation, but one taste of Arabia had ruined him for other women. Too bad their communication skills fell so far short of the sizzling hot chemistry they shared. He'd argued for hours, trying to convince her to accept the damn plea bargain. But the stubborn, contrary-to-the-core woman that she was, Arabia had refused to put her signature on the damn document. And he couldn't, not for the life of him, understand why.

"You thirsty?" Laura poured a shot of his favorite bourbon. She slid it to him.

"That I am." Chase caught the shot glass and took the stool beside Seamus. "Good evening, Mr. District Attorney."

"No need to stand on formalities. It's good to see you, Chase. Thanks for agreeing to meet me outside the office," Grayson said in a thick Irish accent. He offered his hand over the bar top.

The two men exchanged a brisk shake.

"Not a problem. I was stopping here anyway on my way home," Chase said.

Over the course of the last month, he'd taken to passing a couple hours every evening at the Clover Club. He sipped expensive liquor and wallowed in his own misery before heading back to the bed and breakfast where he'd rented a room. Ironically, the bar and the inn felt more like home than the penthouse condominium in LA. Undoubtedly, Grayson knew the ins and outs of Chase's routine. The grizzled old Irishman had his hands on the strings of just about everything that happened in Stillwater, from the supernatural to the secular.

Grayson tipped the brim of his plaid Paddy cap. In keeping with his country gentleman persona, he wore a wool tweed suit and scuffed brown loafers. He carried a pewter-capped cane, which was currently propped against the side of the bar. Grayson uttered his words at a careful, measured pace. "Still, I appreciate it. It was not my goal to inconvenience you in any way."

"You haven't." Chase narrowed his eyes in suspicion. He wasn't fooled for one second. For all his contrived modesty, Seamus Grayson was simply a clever, patient wolf... and a dangerous one because of it. His connections in the wolf-shifter communities reached far and wide, including being legal counsel to the Kohl family of Roanoke. Additionally, Grayson was the grand uncle of Ace Grayson, the Alpha of the Valley of Fire Pack, and grandfather to Gavin Bridges, the Alpha of Stillwater.

Grayson removed a pewter carry case from within the lapel of his suit coat. The moment he opened it, the rich scent of Havana tobacco wafted into the air. "Can I offer you a cigar?"

Involuntarily, Chase drank in a deep inhalation. He might even have tipped toward the delicious aroma, and his fingers twitched despite the line of nicotine patches plastered across his upper arm, hidden beneath his clothing. Craving struck him like the lash of a whip. *Fuck, but he needed a cigarette.* Right that moment, even a cigar would've fit the bill. It required an act of will not to accept the old man's offer.

"Thanks, but I quit." Chase offered a bland smile, baring his teeth.

"Do you mind if I smoke?" Grayson removed a cigar cutter from his coat pocket and trimmed the end. He produced an ornate lighter, poised to strike, and *then* waited for permission.

"Be my guest." Chase sipped his bourbon to stop himself from grinding his teeth. He trod on a veneer of patience that was thin ice beneath a warm sun.

"My thanks." Grayson held the flame to the point of the cigar and drew on the other end until a red ember smoldered at the center. He exhaled, blowing forth a steady stream of smoke.

"What can I do for you, Seamus?" Chase set his shot glass down, gazing down into the amber fluid as it swirled, and settled his forearms against the edge of the counter. The motion drew his suit coat taut across his shoulders. Beneath his clothing and his human skin, his wolf roiled like a restless sea.

Trapped—a prisoner to the material accouterments of the civilized world and the bipedal form he spent far too much of his existence in. His career as an attorney defined him—from his expensive possessions, including that luxury penthouse condo he hardly ever saw, to the eighty-hour workweeks.

His wolf resented it and him.

"I'd like to discuss the plea bargain," Grayson said. "Have you had an opportunity to present our offer to Ms. Jensen?"

"Yep, did that today." Chase polished off the last ounce of his drink and shoved the empty shot glass forward. Reluctance built in his gut, trapped behind a dam of impotent rage. Arabia's stubborn refusal to compromise frustrated him till he wanted to roar. It made him ill—*literally, physically ill*—seeing her caged. His wolf wanted nothing more than to tear down the prison walls and set her free, but the man in him recognized the need to respect rules. He didn't understand why she wouldn't do the reasonable thing and compromise.

"What did she say?" Grayson asked with ill-disguised, unsavory curiosity that was entirely unbecoming in a man of his stature.

"She declined your offer," Chase drawled. For

the sake of civility, he wouldn't repeat Arabia's response, not even to paraphrase.

"Does she understand that it's our final attempt at negotiation?"

"She does."

"And..."

"And it makes no difference. Ms. Jensen prefers to proceed to trial."

"That's unfortunate. Miss Jensen's love spell incited a riot—"

An almost imperceptible growl rolled from Detective Savage. Chase glanced over in time to see the panther-shifter throw back his drink. He smashed down the tumbler. Clearly, Savage had been eavesdropping. The man's anger, however, sparked suspicion in Chase. He wondered if the law enforcement officer had been affected by the love spell.

Of course, every patron in the bar had their acute, preternatural hearing tuned to Grayson and Chase's conversation. Chase understood Seamus's reasons for conducting what should've been a private negotiation in public: To avoid accusations of collusion in a situation that was already political dynamite. Given Detective Savage's reaction, however, Chase had to wonder if there was more to it than that.

Grayson pursed his lips before he concluded. "Inciting a riot is a grave offense."

Chase returned his attention to the conversation. "A citywide orgy may've been riotous, but it hardly qualifies as a riot. The only damage done to private property was to the awning of Bumble Bee Florist, which allegedly collapsed beneath the weight of a bear-shifter who was in congress with—"

"Let's keep this polite. No particulars." Grayson wagged his hand.

"Total damages came to forty-two dollars. I've spoken with Mrs. Bee, the proprietor, and we've already settled out of court," Chase shot back with a practiced scoff. Frankly, he hadn't intended to go into specifics, but he didn't say so. Also, he held the private opinion that the Scottish bear-shifter that'd caused the damage to the awning should've been held financially responsible.

No reasonable person performed carnal acts on a floral store's canopy and expected the canvas to hold.

Grayson jeered. "You bribed Mrs. Bee."

In his natural element, Chase settled into the back and forth that went with tough negotiation. "I offered her an adequate compensation package."

"Can I get you gentlemen a refill?" Laura asked, drifting toward them with a bottle in hand.

Both men fell silent upon the bartender's approach. Laura refilled their glasses and scoured them with her gaze, and then she moved away again. No doubt, her preternatural hearing enabled her to listen in on their conversation. They had to retain at least a semblance of privacy, however, for the negotiation.

Once the bartender departed, Chase waved his hand in a dismissive motion. "Let's not rehash all this again, Seamus. We're wasting our time."

The DA met his stare without blinking. "Let's cut the shit, Chase. The case against your client is ironclad. She's as guilty as sin. If this goes to trial, I intend to prosecute her to the fullest extent of the law. The *only* reason my office even offered a plea bargain in the first place is because Miss Jensen is ravenborn."

"Ravenborn are the favored messengers of the gods." Chase bared his teeth in a wolf's smile—hard and hungry. "Punishing one incurs the risk of divine retribution. Often, the punishment is worse than the mischief the ravenborn perpetuated in the first place. The men pressing charges against her are smart to be afraid."

"Come now," Grayson said with a snort. "That's an old wives' tale, perpetuated by the ravenborn for their own benefit. They hide behind their mystique, evading justice—"

"Are you sure about that?" Chase asked in an ominous voice. "Stillwater doesn't have many ravenborn, so you might not be familiar with their ways. My pack is partnered with the Silverwind Conspiracy. I've *seen* things."

"Vague innuendo—*things*—doesn't intimidate me." Grayson narrowed his eyes. "Your client has been offered a better deal than she deserves. A plea of guilty and a public apology in exchange for time served. She's a fool not to take it."

Chase ground his teeth and nursed his bourbon. Privately, he agreed with Grayson, which was exactly what he'd told Arabia. Hell, he'd wasted hours arguing with her till he was blue in the face, and it hadn't done a lick of good. The stubborn, impossibly contrary woman refused to budge.

"We're all fools to one degree or another." Chase shrugged to demonstrate his nonchalance. Contrived, of course, because he was about the polar opposite of indifferent when it came to Arabia. But the gods knew, the woman had certainly made a chump out of him.

"Harrumph." Grayson wagged his brow. "Given the circumstances, I've requested the case be assigned to Judge Ramses."

"What circumstances?" Chase bit back a curse and took care to conceal his displeasure. Judge Ramses happened to be a sphinx, an extremely rare breed of shifter capable of detecting all lies. Not that Chase would've ever knowingly participated in outright deception in court, but he'd have to take extreme care to make sure Arabia didn't testify.

"You know why." Grayson flashed a smug smile. "Ready to reconsider that plea bargain yet?"

"No." Chase flat-out refused to be intimidated. Having Judge Ramses presiding over the case didn't change his strategy. He meant to keep Arabia off the stand no matter what.

"All right, your call. I can't say I understand your stance. You're a smart man, Chase, a brilliant attorney. Your client's position is all but indefensible. The evidence against her is overwhelming. Her moral character is sketchy. Two of her victims are well-respected members of the Stillwater City Council—"

"I'll be sending subpoenas to both Mr. Wilson and Mr. Desmond. Are your esteemed—*respectably married*—witnesses prepared to testify about how they engaged in extramarital affairs?" Chase hardened himself for a bloodthirsty confrontation. Up until now, he and Grayson had obeyed polite social conventions while conducting their negotiations, but now their gloves were off.

"Be careful, Chase. You'll make enemies."

"Then I'll make enemies."

In his entire life, Chase had never backed down from a fight, and he wasn't about to start now. He took his role as Arabia's self-appointed champion to heart. He'd been bailing her out of some sort of trouble or another since she was a little girl. At times, paranoid suspicion overcame common sense, and he convinced himself that she did it on purpose. Whatever the truth might be, he considered himself her protector.

"I expected you'd say that, which is why the District Attorney's office filed a motion for a closed trial due to special circumstances. Judge Ramses granted it this morning." Grayson tapped his fingers against the bar top.

Chase choked back a curse. He'd banked on the proceeding being conducted in the public eye—the more news coverage, the better. In part, his strategy depended on the whole thing being so embarrassing that those esteemed members of the Stillwater City

Council would back down before allowing it to happen.

"And what special circumstances are *those?*" Chase asked once he recovered his composure. Chagrin was a bitter brew.

"Why, the defendant is a ravenborn princess," Grayson said. "Of course, she must be sheltered from salacious attention while justice is being served."

"Of course." Chase damn near bit through his tongue. He twitched, fingers clenching, on the verge of shifting his hands to claws. It required the entirety of his will not to wipe that smirk from Grayson's smug face.

"Last chance. We can still make a deal."

"My client's refusal is final. We're going to trial."

"Then we're done here." Grayson removed his wallet and placed a bill on the counter to cover his tab. He slid off his bar stool, grasped his cane, and offered his hand. They shook again, and the district attorney left.

Chase hunched over the bar, nursing his drink, while his temper cooled. When Detective Savage approached, Chase twitched but didn't turn. He preferred to avoid another confrontation. A part of him hoped the panther-shifter would just continue on his way.

No such luck.

Savage slid onto the recently vacated barstool. "I'd like a word with you."

"Sure." Chase stifled a sigh and glanced over.

Savage slipped his wallet from his back pocket and extracted two twenties and a five. He laid the bills on the bar and shoved them toward Chase.

"What's this?" Chase glanced at the money but didn't touch it.

"The awning," Savage snarled. A hot flush flooded his face and throat.

"That was you?" Chase tried and failed to keep the surprise off his countenance. His mind acted slowly when it came to putting it together, but the pieces assembled jigsaw fashion. *The awning of the Bumble Bee Florist—a Scottish werebear—and a panther-shifter?!*

"The awning wasn't my idea. I told her it wouldn't hold us." And without excuses or apologies, Savage marched for the exit.

CHAPTER 3

TWO SWANS INN

Following his meeting with Seamus Grayson, Chase headed back to Two Swans Inn, the bed and breakfast that'd been his home for the past month. He hadn't returned to Los Angeles since Arabia's arrest. His loyal assistant, Rose, had shipped the few belongings he needed and made the necessary arrangements to take care of his bills and his houseplants. In his place, his mother and father came out of retirement to assume short-term leadership of the pack.

Beyond a shadow of doubt, his people were safe and watched over, but the knowledge didn't alleviate his guilt in the least. He was, in a phrase, an absent alpha. A day didn't pass in which he didn't worry about their welfare. He wondered what they thought of him—the leader who'd dropped everything to come to the aid of a ravenborn. Gossip must be running rampant through the ranks. When he imagined the wagging tongues—the lascivious speculation—his ears burned.

In the mudroom, Chase shed his winter coat and removed his snow-crusted boots. His sensitive hearing picked up jingling tags, alerting him to the approach of Bonnie and Clyde, the proprietor's purebred German Shepherds.

"It's me." Chase bent and offered his open hand.

As soon as they identified him, both dogs went from aggressive to friendly. Clyde bared his teeth in a doggie-smile of appeasement, wagging his tail frantically. Bonnie conducted herself with more dignity, but she charged straight forward to receive his pats. He talked softly, offering praise and endearments.

"Chase, is that you?" Grant Ward called from the front room.

"Yes, Mr. Ward. It's just me." Chase dropped a final pat onto the heads of the dogs and straightened. He passed through the entryway and past the stairs, with Bonnie and Clyde following on his heels.

The homey main room smelled like old furniture, smoke and ash, and the overpowering scent of peppermints from a tin. Grant Ward occupied a rocking chair before the grand stone fireplace. A graying older man, wiry framed, he wore spectacles and a shawl-collar cardigan. Grant always had a container of Altoids tucked into the front pocket of his sweater. True to his swan-shifter heritage, he had a long neck and his every movement was a study in stately grace.

"You're home late." The old man implied just a touch of criticism.

Mrs. Margaret Ward would've leveled far more pointed censure. Lucky for Chase, the old swan-wife never stayed up past the stroke of midnight. She turned in religiously at eleven thirty every evening. With a cackle, she would declare, "Off to bed with me. It's pumpkin time."

"Yes, sir," Chase said. "Today was long, that's for sure." He leaned against the doorjamb and crossed his arms. It felt good to relax even a tad. He carried enough stress in his neck and shoulders to keep a masseuse busy for a week.

"How's your young lady doing?" Grant extended his hand and snapped his fingers, summoning his dogs. Clyde pushed his muzzle into his master's palm. Bonnie did the same and then sank to the floor at his feet.

For the briefest second, Chase considered evading the question. Arabia wasn't *officially* his lady or even his girlfriend. Hell, he wasn't even sure what they meant to each other. The very lack of definition tormented him. He'd devoted hours trying to figure it—*them*—out and still hadn't arrived at a solid conclusion. He disliked lying, so he simply smiled and said, "She's holding up. Arabia is as stubborn as a mule and twice as ornery."

Grant chuckled. "So is my Maggie, if you can believe that."

"Oh, I can believe it. No challenge there."

The two men shared a quiet laugh. Then Grant lifted his finger. "I just remembered. A man dropped by around noon asking after you."

"Oh?" Chase raised his brow, instilled with a sudden sense of caution. He knew few people in Stillwater, fewer still who'd have knowledge of his lodgings or reason to visit him.

"Yeah, he said his name was John, but he sure didn't look like a John to me. He was a strange sort."

"What'd he look like?"

"Oh, early-to-mid-twenties, gold eyes, straight black hair about so long." Grant indicated his jawline with a slicing motion. "He had a dangerous look about him: all black, lots of chunky runic insignia rings that were pretty obviously enchanted."

"What type of shifter was he?"

Grant shook his head. "That's the funny thing. I couldn't tell, 'n' I've got an instinct for it. Usually, I can call a shifter's breed at a glance. This guy, though..."

Chase's vague unease coalesced into a murky fog of suspicion. "What did this man say?"

"He claimed you and he were old friends from grade school, but you'd lost touch because of a move. He said he'd heard you were in town for the infamous Stillwater Orgy Trial. He wanted to talk to you but didn't know how to get ahold of you."

Chase stroked his finger across his mustache, and pondered for a moment. John was a common enough name, but the man's description didn't ring any bells. "He lied. I don't know this John-guy at all."

"Yup, figured as much." Grant gave a sage nod. "Maggie pegged him as a liar right off the bat. She gets feelings about folks."

"Anything else I should know?"

"Nothing of consequence. He asked a few more questions about you, but we didn't tell him anything. After a while, he got frustrated and left in a huff."

"If he comes around again, call the police." Chase

disliked the prospect of the stranger being around the elderly couple. He had a bad feeling lodged in his gut.

Grant nodded. "Will do."

Chase stifled a yawn against his fist. He needed sleep in a desperate way, and he was going to be darn lucky if he made it up the stairs without falling flat on his face. "Good night, Grant."

Grant chuckled. "G'night yourself."

CHAPTER 4

SEXCAPADES EXPLAINED

December 6th...

Officer Nelson swung the reinforced security door open and gestured Arabia through. The female guard was a surly old fart who had the build of a power lifter and a reputation for roughing up prisoners who 'had it coming'.

"You have a half-hour," Nelson said.

"Thanks." Arabia looked sharp and stepped fast while she passed through the entrance, taking care to avoid accidental contact with the woman.

After the security door banged shut, Arabia turned away. The prison's visitation center was surprisingly crowded for a Thursday morning. She wasn't expecting anyone today, and Officer Nelson had refused to disclose the identity of Arabia's guest.

Her family visited on weekends, but that was still a couple days off. When Chase called, they always met in one of the conference rooms provided specifically for attorney-client meetings.

Anticipation had her twitchier than a long-tailed cat in a roomful of rocking chairs. The visitation center was a spacious cavern that was always too cold or too hot. The furnishings consisted of particleboard tables and molded plastic chairs. There was a children's area with two beaten-down beanbags, and a battered pile of books and puzzles that looked like they needed CDC germ warning labels.

She scanned the area, searching for a familiar—hopefully friendly—face in the sea of strangers. Speculation ran rampant through her imagination in a wild guessing game of who-could-it-be? Maybe that jerkoff District Attorney had experienced an unexpected epiphany about the sheer wrongheadedness of his ways? He wished to apologize in person and say he was dropping the charges? A cynical snort gathered in Arabia's throat. Yeah, right. If she bought into that wistful thinking, it was time to invest in Florida real estate.

Arabia harbored no idea who her mystery caller might be, but surprise still managed to knock her off balance. Her lips parted in faint surprise when her gaze landed on the only person in the room who was both alone and she recognized.

Penelope Reed was a librarian, a werewolf, and also a former client. Arabia had performed readings for Penny in the past. They weren't friends, though, and didn't run in the same social circles. Arabia suspected Penny probably hadn't told any of her friends or colleagues that she consulted a witch on a regular basis. Penny wasn't the *last* person Arabia would've expected to visit her in prison, but the librarian ranked pretty low on the list.

Penny smiled faintly and whispered, "Hi, there."

Arabia's hand rose to her chest. She almost returned, "Me?" but it was just too much of a cliché. Instead, she shuffled over to where Penny occupied a table beside the vending machines.

Penny perched on the edge of her seat, legs angled to the side because of her pencil skirt. She maintained a ruler-straight posture as though to keep physical contact with the chair to a bare minimum. The statuesque brunette pretty much personified what a stereotypical 'repressed sexy librarian' ought to look like: long dark-brown hair pulled back in a severe ponytail, a white silk blouse, black skirt, and sensible heels. The only missing element was eyewear, and Arabia would've bet her last dollar that Penny had a pair of reading glasses tucked away somewhere.

Penny's body language telegraphed discomfort. Oh boy, here was a woman who'd rather be anywhere else. It really begged the question—what was so important that Penny had risked coming to such an alien environment? Arabia's gut feeling said the librarian's reasons probably had to do with the Heart's Desire spell... and the so-called orgy that had followed.

This ought'a be interesting.

Arabia mustered a polite, maybe overly bright smile to cover her anxiety. "Hi, Penny. It's been a while. Are you here to see me?"

"Yes. Please have a seat," Penny said with stiff formality. She gestured to the chair opposite her, calling attention to the shininess of her French manicure.

A hornet of envy buzzed through Arabia, and a swarm of self-consciousness followed—everything about Penny screamed perfection, whereas Arabia epitomized grunginess. She tried telling herself that her wretched appearance wasn't her fault, but it did nothing to alleviate her embarrassment. Her attempts to dismiss the feelings of inadequacy failed.

Arabia sat carefully, also perching. She cleared her throat and asked, "So, how've you been?"

Penny kept smiling. "Good. And you?"

"Not quite good, but you know us raven-shifters. We're adaptable."

"That's good."

They shared an awkward sound that fell short of a laugh. *Attempted laughter.* Arabia sure as hell hoped she couldn't be charged for murdering humor, too. In vexation, she huffed. "Well, it sounds like everything's good."

Unconformable silence fell.

Penny smoothed her already wrinkle-free skirt. Arabia sighed. Oops, she'd overdone the sarcasm and killed the goodness. The women stared at each other, waiting for something to happen, and time dragged on.

Arabia's patience ran out first. No surprises there. As ravens proved prone to do, she launched into chatter. "I hope you don't need a reading. I don't have my cards on me."

"Well..." Penny gulped.

"Go ahead." Arabia tensed, clenching her hands. She braced. *Here it comes...*

"Is it true that you used a love spell that night when the whole city went crazy?" Penny spat out.

Even though she'd expected it, the question still hit Arabia like a blow. She winced a bit and skewed her face up. The briefest inkling to lie crossed her mind. Deny everything and disavow all knowledge. But that wouldn't be fair to Penny. And Chase's rebuke about Arabia's failure to take responsibility for her actions remained fresh in her mind. She wanted to earn his respect, which meant making an effort to change.

Well, here was her opportunity.

Arabia took a deep breath. "Yes, I cast a spell the night the whole city went crazy."

Penny inhaled sharply.

"But there are a couple big buts..." Arabia talked fast, determined to get her explanation in. She fully expected to make the other woman angry. Penny might be the world's second most buttoned down werewolf—right after Chase. No matter how conservative, though, a pissed off wolf still had teeth and the instinct to bite. "First, it was a heart's desire incantation, not a love spell."

Penny frowned. "I'm not sure I know what that means."

"I can explain if you're willing to listen."

"I'm listening." Penny crossed her arms beneath her breasts.

"This is what it means. Love spells are ranked right up there with hexes for a lot of witches, including me. The removal of free will is a red-hot no-no. A Heart's Desire spell strips away fears and doubts, but only for one night. The magic frees lovers from inhibitions and reveals secret attractions. Despite what people are claiming, no one was coerced into falling for anyone they weren't already drawn to. Or slept with anyone they didn't truly want."

"You mentioned there are a few *buts*."

Arabia blinked and delayed. For a second, she'd forgotten her other points but they returned to her quickly. "Oh. I cast the spell into a potion. It had to be imbibed through a sip of wine. It was only supposed to affect me and the man I shared the potion with."

"So what happened? How'd it result in citywide sexcapades?"

A hot blush swept over Arabia. She shook her head slowly and spread her hands. "None of what happened makes any sense at all. It shouldn't have swept through the entire town the way it did."

"Except it did." Penny scowling, looking pained, and it probably had nothing to do with the awful chair.

The ravenborn knit her brow. Confusion filled her, because this part defied her understanding. Next, Arabia's mind flitted to the evening in question. Hmm, should she mention the six extra drops of divine essence she'd added to the potion? Was it too damning? She pondered and decided. *Yeah, way too damning.* It qualified as one of those secrets meant to be taken to one's grave—*her* grave in this particular case.

Arabia did her best to explain, only with an abbreviated version. "That night, something went terribly wrong. The enchantment was way more powerful and widespread than it should have been. Believe me, I researched *everything* prior to casting it—potential consequences, the effects of ley lines and moon phases. It was only meant to affect the two of us... I've been locked up since it happened so I haven't had a chance to investigate."

"I'm not sure that's helpful."

Fifteen minutes had passed. They still had time. Curiosity was just killing her, so Arabia decided to ask some nosy questions. "I'm sorry. It might help if I understood why you're asking. Tell me and maybe I can help."

Penny licked her lips. Hesitantly, she began,

"Something happened to me that night. Something I'd never in a million years imagined *could* occur..."

A broad grin split Arabia's mouth. "You don't say?"

"I kind of had sex with a stranger, and that's not like me at all. I mean, it isn't like I don't like sex, because I do, a lot, but a one-night stand with someone I just met? No way I'd do something like that."

"Whoa!" Arabia's sly smile dropped and her eyes widened. She pondered, and her expression grew more thoughtful. "So, there's no way you'd do something like that. Except you did do it. So now you want to blame it on the magic, huh? Or maybe me?"

"Maybe your potion changed me? I don't know. I can't think of a reality where I'd go to bed with a complete stranger. And a shifter at that..." A faraway look crossed Penny's face, and she seemed to become lost in memory.

"Since you didn't drink my potion, I don't see how," Arabia said, but she was positive the werewolf didn't hear her.

Out of the blue, Penny said, "It went on the whole night. It was insane."

An awful thought occurred to Arabia. She recoiled in horror and then placed a sympathetic hand on Penny's wrist. "Oh goddess, was it bad? Didn't you enjoy yourself?"

Penny jutted her chin. "He was great. More than great, but that's not why I came here to talk to you. What I'm trying to understand is how I became a slut overnight."

Arabia almost swallowed her tongue. She dropped her voice to a whisper-hiss. "Don't you dare slut-shame yourself!"

Penny took a long breath. She pulled her arm free from Arabia's grasp and flattened her hand against the table. After staring at her manicured nails for an overly long time, she tilted her chin up again. "My upbringing was quite strict. I might have mentioned my very religious family once or twice during our sessions."

Arabia pressed her lips together. She had to bite her tongue and strove for a neutral tone. "I remember you saying that."

"It's hard to break the mold."

Arabia grimaced. "I get it. I do. Ravenborn have a reputation as thieves and tricksters. Sometimes it's easier to be what people expect you to be than what you want." She fell silent, pondering. Self-honesty sucked big time. She hated it.

Time to bounce back into character...

"But hey!" Arabia said. "You had a hot one-night stand with a hot, ripped dude. You've totally broken the mold."

Penny blushed red-hot.

"Do you think about that night a lot? I can tell you're thinking about him right now, aren't cha?" Arabia chided with a wink-nod.

Penny tapped her fingernails on the table. "Yes, I do think of him."

"Like a little or a lot?"

Penny's self-deprecatory scoff would've served as answer enough, but she went on. "A lot. I can't think of anything else. I can't sleep. I can't eat. I want him in my bed, again. And again. And again. It's like a fever."

"Wow." Arabia grinned from ear-to-ear. *Cheshire Cat, eat your heart out!*

Shaking her head, Penny laughed. "This librarian's dirty thoughts would make a seasoned porn star blush."

Arabia bit the insides of her cheeks. She wanted to snicker, but poor Penny was so serious and upset. Laughing seemed too cruel. "So, you have fantasies, huh?"

"Yeah. But I would never act on them. But it's

okay to think about them. That's what fantasies are for, right?"

A snort ripped from her throat. "Right. Except you did act on them already. I hate to break this to you, but all the heart's desire spell did was free you to be yourself. You can google the incantation if you don't believe me."

Penny fixed a long, hard stare on the raven-shifter. When the librarian finally spoke, her voice emerged strained. "So you're saying the spell only unleashed the real me?"

"It was all you. The incredible one-night stand fantasy woman."

Penny trembled like a bedraggled kitten. She whispered, "What about him?"

"What about him?" Arabia cocked her head.

"Did he really want to have sex with me?"

"Of course he did." Arabia crushed the impulse to scoff, because mocking another person's misery wasn't her style. Honestly, though, Penny's uncertainty was both heartbreaking and crazy-making. For the love of silly things, the wolf-shifter was gorgeous! How could she not know?

Penny folded her arms again. "Well, that's good to know, I guess. At least, he wanted me as much as I wanted him."

Arabia started to speak, but she missed the opening.

"What do you think I should do now?" Penny asked.

"Is that a trick question? I can tell you what I'd do in your shoes, but what you need is to figure out what you want. Have you tried talking to him?"

The werewolf shook her head, sending her ponytail flying. "Of course not! I can't even look at him and not remember the things we did that night. When we met by chance, I could barely breathe."

Oh brother.

Arabia thanked her lucky stars she hadn't been born timid. When she answered, she strove to sound patient. "You need to talk to him,"

"And what if I can't do it"?

"Then you'll spend the rest of your life alone and full of regrets. I'm sorry. I don't want to be mean but the truth is harsh. That man is your soulmate. The spell may've revealed an inconvenient truth and freed you from fear for one night, but that's all it did. The rest is up to you."

Arabia composed a mental prayer to Ceridwen, asking the goddess to bestow her blessing upon Penny and her enigmatic lover. Arabia had far too many doubts to assume even for a second that everything would work out for her and Chase. For the sake of karma, someone needed to have a happily ever after.

"I wish you could read my future, but thank you for speaking to me so frankly."

"You're welcome. Good luck."

Penny's visit bothered Arabia all day long. She replayed their conversation in her head over and over. The encounter had upset her more than she realized. Even after she began to grasp the depths of her unrest, the reasons for the underlying tension eluded her.

At lights out, she crawled into her uncomfortable bunk with dread and anticipation. She vowed to remain awake, and insomnia often made it an easy promise to keep. For hours, she stared into darkness, fretting, full of regret and fear. She revisited every unwise decision she'd made, including the one that'd landed her behind bars. Second-guessed the whole thing—whether she ought to have accepted that plea bargain—and worried that she'd never again know freedom.

Eventually, inevitably, exhaustion weighted her

eyelids until she wasn't strong enough to keep them open anymore. They shut, and she dropped straight into a deep slumber. Even her sleep wasn't peaceful.

Vivid memories haunted and tormented her. In dreams, she relived the bliss of Chase's embrace, opened herself to love and longing, and they were together again. At dawn, alarms blared through the prison and jarred her from her reverie. She awakened alone with the warmth of his scent lingering in her nostrils. The passion of his embrace in her thoughts... She sat up abruptly in her bunk, arms wrapped tightly around her torso, trying to hold onto the fantasy.

Emptiness awaited her. Lifetime imprisonment. The huge and terrible consequences seemed almost impossible to believe, considering how this had all started out with a harmless little lie...

WOLF BAITING

One month prior—November 7th...

The bang of a car door closing grabbed Arabia's attention. Through the front window of her cozy bungalow, she spied a sedan parked curbside. Overhead, the silvery winter moon hung so low in the sky it seemed to perch atop the mountainous skyline. A formidable dark-haired man climbed from the driver's seat, ducking his head to evade the grasping frosty fingers of the snow-laden tree that bordered the sidewalk.

Chase had come at last!

Her heart thumped and smashed, first in her throat and then mightily against her chest. She froze in eagle-eyed readiness, clutching the drinking glass she'd meant to load into the dishwasher. The faucet kept running and water poured down the drain, but her gaze stayed glued to Chase while he rounded his vehicle and strolled up the front sidewalk.

The solid rap of knuckles on the front door announced his arrival—the man Arabia had been waiting for her entire life. It jarred her from her trancelike state of rapt fascination. She placed the glass into the top rack, shoved the dishwasher closed, and shut off the faucet.

"Coming!" She raced on feet so swift and light she practically flew. She burst through the beaded curtain in the archway at full speed, setting the glass beads to clinking together in a cheerful clatter. As a raven, she loved bright, shiny things. It also served a practical purpose: separating the front room where she saw the clients of her apothecary and herbal healing business from her personal living area. She also read palms and tarot cards, crafted astrological forecasts, and cleansed auras. Jack of all trades—a little bit of this and that—whatever it took to pay the rent.

A second knock, just as hard and demanding as the man himself, came just as she closed her hand on the knob. She stopped, panting heavily, and forced herself to slow down. Giving herself a mental pat on the back, she muttered, "You've got this."

The door swung open, revealing Chase with his fist raised. For a moment, absolute silence hung between them. He stared—she stared. It'd been two years since she'd last laid eyes on the man, but Arabia swore he'd only gotten handsomer.

"Hello, Arabia," Chase said in a husky voice. The corners of his mouth lifted in a tentative smile. He wore a winter coat and a gray three-piece suit. Stereotypically Southern California, the man had a healthy tan even in the dead of winter.

Arabia *meant* to offer Chase a polite greeting. She'd rehearsed their reunion in front of the mirror dozens of times, planning for every contingency. For everything he might say, she had an answer prepared. She would be cool and collected... so utterly grown up... that Chase's respect for her would skyrocket. But the moment she got close to him, Arabia forgot herself. Excitement surged through her, and her poise sailed right out the window, taking all her fancy-pants plans with it.

"Chase!" With a cry of joy, Arabia flew straight at him. She collided with his solid chest, locked her hands against his nape, and clung for dear life.

"Wow." Chase released a gust of surprise. His arms came around her; his strength sheltered her. The rightness was impossible to describe. If, somewhere in the world, a word existed that meant 'I belong in your embrace', Arabia would've loved to learn it.

"Wow?" Arabia echoed, and found the exclamation matched the smashing sensation of having been bowled over to a T. She buried her face against his throat and inhaled, drinking in his toasty warmth.

Chase inhaled and his breath tugged at her loose locks. The casual intimacy of the gesture thrilled her to the depths of her silly corvid toes. "Yeah, I figured you wouldn't be thrilled to have *me* turn up on your doorstep."

Stop! She scolded herself and recited sensible explanations—wolves possessed an innate fixation on scent. Chase was only doing what came natural to him. There was nothing special about it. Really, she ought to consider herself lucky that he hadn't sniffed her butt. Or maybe, just maybe—a devilish smile curved her lips—she should offer to bend over.

"Don't be silly. It's just been so long since I've seen anyone from home." The hug had to end. It'd already gone on too long for a spontaneous display of affection between long lost friends.

It took all her willpower, but Arabia pried her interlaced fingers apart and released her cinch hold on the back of Chase's neck. After a slight delay, he loosened his arms. She slid down his chest and alighted on her feet. The icy porch boards creaked softly.

Awkwardness filled up the space between them. Chase loomed larger than life. For all the time she'd spent fantasizing about this moment, she found herself paralyzed with indecision now that he'd arrived. At a loss, Arabia stroked the front of her lace-up corset, brushing off imaginary lint. Abruptly, she became aware of the frigid evening air and started shivering.

Chase blew out, and his breath formed a dense finger of fog that streamed past her face. "Are you going to invite me in?"

She stepped aside and gestured for him to enter. "Yes, of course. Please come inside."

Chase raised his arm and shepherded her through the entryway. "Ladies first."

She went, quelling a joke about his suppressed herding instincts. According to Arabia's father, who was a renowned storyteller with countless tales of ever-expanding fish, Chase's great-great-*great*-grandfather had mated and married a cattle dog-shifter about the same time the Baron Pack had claimed their Southern California territory. To this day, it remained a touchy subject with the wolves.

Fido-go-fetch jokes had gotten old.

Chase entered the parlor and closed the front door behind him. He stopped beside the round oak table Arabia used to perform divinations for her clients. And, as wolves were wont to do, he adopted an alert stance—head held high, legs planted wide. He assessed his surroundings in an instinctive search for potential threats.

"Can I take your coat?" She aimed a pointed stare at his feet. A slushy crust clung to his leather loafers. It'd already begun to melt, spreading about him to form a muddy puddle.

"Thanks." He shrugged out of his coat. As he passed it to her, their fingers brushed, sending exhilarating tingles along her nerve endings. With just a touch, he brought her alive in an incredible way. In his absence, she lived in a desert of deprivation. She'd dated other men, but not a single one had ever proven capable of filling the special place inside her that only he could reach.

"You're welcome." Arabia smiled and tossed his jacket over a hook on the wrought iron coat rack. She gestured to a chair. "Have a seat. Can I get you something to drink?"

He remained standing and glanced around the small front room. "I'm fine, thank you."

Arabia clasped her hands together to stop fidgeting. She sensed him judging the shabby-chic decor... and by default, her. As long as she'd known the man—basically, her entire life—never once had she lived up to his refined standards.

"What do you think?" Arabia asked and winced at her overly defensive tone.

His guarded gaze flickered to her. "It's nice. Homey."

"It is?" Her voice pitched high, and guilt pinched at her for assuming the worst of him. "I mean... yeah, it is. Thanks."

"You look like you've settled in here." Oddly, Chase sounded less than thrilled. Perhaps he believed she meant to remain in Stillwater, and the prospect displeased him. Hope sprang eternal in her raven heart, and it took a real effort to stop leaping to all sorts of other optimistic conclusions.

"I've made some friends, and I have regular clients." Arabia strove to keep calm. "Plus, Stillwater is located at the nexus of powerful ley lines. Magic gets a natural boost here."

"Have you completed your Launching?" Chase

placed emphasis on the question, as though a lot rode on her answer.

"Not quite yet, but I believe my journey is nearing its end," Arabia said warily. "Why do you ask?"

Launching was the ravenborn rite of passage ceremony, which marked their transition from youth to adulthood. At nineteen, Arabia had left her home to wander the world. As was customary, she'd avoided her family and friends, and sought out new relationships. Her journey would continue until she found her life path—to return home, to join another conspiracy, or to keep traveling. Or when she chose a mate. Now twenty-one, she'd grown weary and lonely. She missed her loved ones, the companionship of her conspiracy— and a particular stubborn werewolf—with all her heart.

Chase stayed silent a little too long. Arabia hung on the hook of anticipation, waiting on his answer. Crushing disappointment overtook her when he cleared his throat and said, "No reason."

"So you're just making small talk?" She arched her brow, disgusted with herself for getting her hopes up... and him for failing her.

"I haven't seen you in two years. I care what you've been up to." Chase adopted his best sad-puppy mien, the one she recalled from their misspent youths. That look melted her icy disdain now every bit as effectively as it had then.

"Uh, thanks."

He stepped closer, invading her space; his heat washed over her skin. "Aren't you going to ask why I'm here?"

Arabia jerked and almost retreated. She held her ground, refusing to yield because wolves interpreted submission as weakness. "I figured you'd tell me. But yeah, sure. Why are you here?"

"I figured you'd tell me."

"I'm sorry? I don't understand." His proximity threw her, short-circuited her reason centers, and made her nerves go haywire. She gulped and retrenched, bolstering her defenses.

"I believe you do understand... just like I know you were expecting me."

Arabia cocked her head. "Sorry, I'm not following. Are you implying I had something to do with you coming here?"

"I'm not implying. I'm stating it." Chase drawled and regarded her from beneath a hooded gaze. No surprise or pleasure. Privately, she called that stoicism his legal-eagle face; although, that too-serious expression predated his law degree by years.

"Wow, that sounds a bit paranoid, don't you think?" Arabia asked with confidence that her ravenborn magic would allow her to evade even a werewolf's ability to smell lies. *Of course*, she had conspired to bring Chase to her. He could suspect all he wanted, but he couldn't *know* for sure. Arabia had taken great care to cover her trail.

"If it was anyone other than you, I'd probably agree." Chase radiated crackling readiness—an air of anticipation that tickled her tail feathers. He'd changed. The Chase she'd known would've engaged in a blunt confrontation and demanded answers. Even as a child, he'd pursued his goals with dogged determination. This man, the one before her now, struck her as more circumspect. It worried her, because it meant he was unpredictable.

It thrilled her, too.

Arabia fluttered her lashes in practiced flirtation. "Fine, I'll play along. Theoretically, suppose I did lure you to this isolated town in the middle of nowhere. What would be my motivation?"

"Theoretically?" He flashed a hungry smile, and her gut quivered with delicious trepidation. Arabia had to stop a moment and remind herself that wolves and ravens hunted as partners. She wasn't on the menu... unless she chose to put herself there.

With a practiced flip, she tossed her hair over her shoulder. "Theoretically... what do I gain?"

Chase tracked her every movement with predatory intensity. "Other than the pleasure of yanking my chain? I assume you want something from me."

She grinned. "Yanking your chain is always fun, but I'd have to have a better reason than that to go to all the trouble of luring you here."

He smiled in return. "Which brings us back to the wanting."

"Ah, I see how it is, counselor. What is it exactly that you suppose I want?" Arabia swept his muscular physique with a thorough up-down assessment, leaving no room for doubt.

Chase hesitated. Doubt crossed his handsome face, and she huffed in impatience. She *wanted* to shout for him to stop being so damn intellectual. He should trust his instincts. Chase must know how much she adored him—how she'd been infatuated with him her entire life.

Fear kept her silent.

To her vast disappointment, rationality won out. Chase said, "You called Reidar for help."

With a grunt, Arabia perched on the edge of the table. Fine—he wanted the game to continue? She'd play. "That's right. I called *Reidar*, my brother. That doesn't explain what you're doing here."

"Reidar's in Australia on business. He asked me to check on you." Chase narrowed his eyes, his jawline set in stone. "So, what's wrong?"

"Nothing."

"Nothing? You're telling me I dropped everything and drove hundreds of miles because everything is okay?"

"A, I didn't ask you to come." She snapped up one finger, and then a second. "B, you could've called."

"I tried to call. I left messages."

"Didn't get them." Technically it was the truth. She hadn't checked her messages since she'd left her emergency message on Reidar's voicemail. It gave her plausible deniability and all that.

He hefted a skeptical brow. "That so?"

Arabia smiled and rolled her shoulders. "Sure is. My cell service sucks. We're on the edge of town here. Most days I'm lucky to have two bars, depending on which way the wind is blowing. I'll probably get them next week."

"All right." He nodded but his tone said things were anything but. He didn't like her explanation—not one bit. "So what's wrong?"

"I told you. It was nothing. I overreacted and did

what I always do when things get tough—went running straight to my big brother. It's a bad habit. I realized what I'd done as soon as I hung up, so I called him back and told him to never mind. Didn't Reidar get that message, too?"

"He got it."

"He didn't believe it, huh?" She arched her brow in a pointed challenge.

"That's between you and Reidar." Chase sidestepped the issue with practiced finesse. "I'm here now, so you might as well let me help."

"I told you, I don't need help. It was nothing."

"If it was nothing, then it shouldn't be such a big deal to explain it to me." He exuded the thick musk of testosterone, the super-potent variety that would've busted the balls of a less alpha male. As a raven-shifter, she wasn't as responsive to scents as some others, but the heady aroma got her high. She resisted the urge to tilt toward him and breathe in deep, drinking him in.

Arabia pinned him with an unwavering stare. "You seem to be missing the finer point here, Chase *Earl*"—she pronounced it *hurl*—"Baron. My business is none of your business."

A ferocious scowl stormed his handsome face. Chase *despised* his middle name with a fiery passion.

He guarded his second name like a dirty secret. Professionally, he used his middle initial, which appeared on all his legal documents except his birth certificate. No one outside of his immediate family and closest friends even knew what that E stood for. According to family legend, Chase's mother had insisted on Earl over his father's protests. Beverly Baron: a sadistic, sarcastic, wonderful woman Arabia adored above all other prospective mothers-in-law in the whole wide world. Bev's sheer awesomeness exceeded measurement.

"What's your game?" Chase jutted his strong jaw, but he persisted, ignoring her attempt to bait him.

She threw up her hands. "Gah! Where do you get off? This isn't a game!"

"Everything is a game with you, Arabia." The way he said her name implied intimacy, but the hardened gleam in his eyes conveyed a pointed challenge.

Oh, the man knew her well. Too well. Their entire lives, they'd clashed. As far back as she remembered, even as a girl, she'd crafted elaborate illusions and ingenious trickery, hoping to impress him. Chase was her first crush... her first love. Yet nothing she did garnered more than suspicion or irritation from him.

"I don't know what you're talking about. It's sweet that you're willing to give me so much credit for being clever." Arabia mustered a bright, carefree smile. "I called Reidar for help, Chase. *Reidar*, not you. And immediately afterward, the second I hung up, I called him back and told him never mind. I had no way of knowing he'd be in Australia or that you'd come in his place. You being here isn't part of some elaborate scheme—"

"We're going in circles. Let's cut—"

"To the chase?" She smirked.

"The shit."

She snorted. "How apropos."

"Tell me why you called Reidar for help. Please?"

"Fine, but only because you asked nicely." She exhaled in loud exasperation. "I had a bit of trouble with a warlock from my Pilates class—"

"What's his name?" Chase grew resolved. His eyes glimmered like goldstones within the hard lines of his face.

"That doesn't matter."

"Tell me who he is. I'll deal with him." The deadly intensity of his tone sent shivers coursing down her spine. His fierce protectiveness delighted her to no end.

"No. You'll pull some heavy-handed bullshit and

hurt him. It's fine now. I told him I don't want to see him anymore." She took care to school her face to indifference. Chase might be as handsome as the devil, but he was every bit as smart, too. Even the slightest screw up on her part would clue him in to the game.

After a delay, Chase's frown blossomed to an outright scowl. "You were dating this asshole?"

"Yes, and before you open your mouth..." Arabia aimed her finger at him. "Shut it. I'm a full-grown woman now. I date who I want, when I want. And I don't need yours or my dear older brother's permission."

Thunderous quiet filled the room. Chase's jaws worked. He looked mad enough to chew steel and spit out nails. The man didn't like being put in his place. Not one bit. He undertook an entire journey right before her eyes, progressing from irritation through confusion, but then looped right back to annoyance. His brow knit and his chin jutted.

"I'm not leaving until you tell me his name, *Princess*."

Oohh, Princess. The kid gloves were off now. Chase only resorted to using her title when he got seriously annoyed. To further his point, he pulled out the chair across from her and planted himself in it like a territorial marker. With a great huff, he crossed his arms over his broad chest. The message was clear—he wouldn't budge until he got his way.

She dissolved into giggles, and then laughed harder when he twitched. Surprise blasted away his stubborn resolve. He parted his lips and lifted his hands. Arabia shook her head and slid to her feet. Swiftly, she circled the table to stand beside him and settled her hand on his arm.

"Chase, sweetie, what makes you think I want you gone, especially after all the trouble I *allegedly* went to in order to get you here?" Arabia asked, trailing her fingers across his shoulder. Beneath her touch, he thrummed with tension.

"Arabia..." He cocked his head to the side and narrowed his eyes, regarding her warily. Poor guy, so damn confused. He just didn't know what to make of grown-up Arabia Jensen.

"Yeah, Big B?"

"Don't call me that." He growled, and gold shimmered in the whites of his eyes. Ah, there he was—her wolf, a magnificent, dangerous predator. Warm satisfaction spread through her center like a shot of aged whiskey.

She pouted. "But I've always called you that."

He flashed all his teeth, not smiling or snarling, but a grimace halfway in between. "I know."

"I see no reason to stop now." In a smooth motion, Arabia threw a leg over his lap and straddled him. She grasped his powerful shoulders and dug her nails into his iron-hard muscles.

"What're you doing?" Chase sucked in a sharp breath. He rustled restlessly beneath her.

"What does it look like I'm doing?" She snickered, reveling in the brawny press of his thighs beneath her. A helluva sublime mount, she intended to ride him hard and long. To secure her perch, she hooked her hands behind his neck, fingers interlaced.

"This isn't why I came here." He seized her upper arms but didn't shove her away. His hands betrayed him, kneading her shoulders through her top.

"No?" She spread her thighs wider and scooted closer. He lifted toward her, closing the final bit of space that separated them. Her breasts pressed against his ripped pecs.

"No. It's not, but fuck, you're beautiful." Chase ducked his head but stopped a millimeter shy of kissing her. He wore the tormented look of a man on the edge of his sanity.

Her smile broadened while her fingers fiddled with the short locks of his hair against his nape. She loved seeing Chase Baron—Mr. Calm, Cool, and Collected—coming unraveled. The proof of her power over him tented the front of his pants. The rush went straight to her head.

"It's past time you finally noticed. I want you, Chase Baron. I've wanted you for years. I want you to rip my clothes off, shove me against that wall, and fuck me so hard I scream." She exhaled, blowing a kiss to his lips, and then leaned against him, rubbing her breasts against his chest.

She totally rocked the Goth look, and her current outfit had been chosen with an eye for seduction. Her low-cut blouse showed off her pert breasts that her black corset pushed ever so high. She wore a red plaid minuscule bubble skirt over fishnet stockings and black boots. All he needed to do was hike her skirt, rip off her panties, and he'd be home free.

"Arabia..." Chase frowned and opened his mouth, struggling for the words that seemed to elude him. Oh, she knew the man only too well. As soon as he overcame the mental disruption she'd caused, he'd extricate himself. In his authoritative way, he'd talk down to her, telling her to stop. That this wasn't appropriate. She must be confused or making a terrible mistake. No confrontation or confession as to his own desires. The man kept his cards tucked to his chest, never showing his hand to anyone.

Determined to decimate his defenses, Arabia swooped in and took a teasing nip at his lower lip and then flicked her tongue over the spot. She claimed him for a rough, passionate kiss. The sweetest thing—the way their mouths clung together. She stabbed her tongue into the sultry recesses of his mouth. His skin was hot and dry. He tasted of salt and pepper. Spicy: a concentrated and intense flavor not for the faint of heart.

A growl rumbled in his throat. Chase gripped her shoulders with his big hands. The silly man probably sought to push her away, but desire got the better of him. The balance of power swayed, tipping toward him, and he seized control of the kiss. Rough in his need, he hauled her to him, crushing her breasts against his chest. The friction agitated her hard nipples.

She whimpered and arched toward him, aching for his touch. The five o'clock shadow on his jaw pricked her skin. He delved into her mouth with his tongue, stroked the slickness of her teeth, and caressed the roof of her mouth.

They dueled, the give and take of lunge and parry, a dance for dominance. It went on for seconds, maybe even hours, and Arabia lost all connection with reality. Her blood burned, roaring in her ears, and pressure built in her chest till she thought she would explode. With the same volatile force that'd brought them together, they separated to gasp for air.

Their gazes collided and locked, Chase's handsome face set into a stony mask. Best guess, he expected her to say something. Worst-case scenario, he dreaded what that might be. For her part, Arabia found herself at an absolute loss. She made a sound in the back of her throat, unable to formulate words. For well over a decade, she'd dreamt about what it'd be like to kiss Chase Baron. Even her grandest fantasy fell short of the reality.

As greedy as a child in a candy store, she leaned in, going back for more, but he caught her shoulders. "Wait, slow down. What's happening here?"

"Mmm, if I have to explain, you're not the man I thought." She writhed against him, using her curves to fight dirty.

Chase groaned. "Arabia, this isn't right."

Anger flared as brilliant as a supernova in her core. With a cry of frustration, Arabia slid off his lap, landing square on her feet. For many long years she'd wanted this infuriating man—longed for him, ached for him, *burned* for him. And he desired her in return. The proof was in his pants. They were both adults now, so why, then—*why?*—did he persist in denying them?

"Fine, you leave me no other choice," Arabia said. "We'll do this the hard way."

"Good. Everything will be fine once we talk about this," Chase agreed with heartfelt enthusiasm, wiping perspiration off his brow.

"I could use a drink. What about you?" Arabia asked.

"Yeah, I think I'm ready for that drink now." Relief lightened his expression and tone because he believed—quite wrongly—she meant to be reasonable.

Poor man, he had no clue.

Screw talking—and screw reason.

Plan A, Wolf Baiting, might've failed, but she refused to admit defeat. Failure was naught but a temporary setback. Upward and onward to Plan B!

Love Potion No. 9.

CHAPTER 6

November 7th...

Arabia squared her shoulders with renewed determination. She adopted a casual air, acting for all she was worth. Chase needed to believe that what'd just happened between them hadn't affected her at all. If he suspected the true extent of her frustration, he'd follow her into the kitchen. She couldn't have that; her backup plan required a couple minutes of privacy.

"I have wine. Do you prefer red wine or white?" She gazed into the pewter-framed mirror mounted on the wall.

Red lipstick smudged her upper lip. She removed it with a quick swipe of her fingertip. Hastily, she finger-combed her hair and touched the warmth of the solid gold hair bead that anchored the single braid that dangled over her shoulder. A pleased smile curved her lips, and she stroked the ornate details etched on the surface. The decoration was new, she'd only owned it for a week or so, and she sometimes forgot it was there.

"Red, thank you. Do you need help?" Ironically, Chase sounded shaken to the core. *That kiss...* Good to know she wasn't the only one whose world had been rocked.

"Help with what?" She pivoted toward where he remained seated.

"Opening the bottle?" Chase grinned, and an indentation appeared on his cheek close to the corner of his mouth. She loved that dimple, so warm and inviting... A shame he didn't smile more often.

She snorted. "Are you serious? I can open a bottle of wine all on my lonesome. Is that how those Hollywood bleached blondes are—too helpless to operate a corkscrew without a man's help?"

"I wouldn't know," he said with a husky chuckle. "I prefer brainy, well-spoken brunettes."

Then I should be right up your alley. I'm a sass act all the way. Arabia bit her tongue to hold back the catty remark. Instead, she just smiled. "I'll be right back. Try out the leather armchair by the fireplace. Put your feet up."

"Thanks, maybe I will." Chase approached the armchair with a wolf's innate wariness as if it were a trap waiting to be sprung. No doubt, he suspected her of trickery. Smart man, but his instincts were pointed in the wrong direction.

"Relax, Big B. It doesn't bite."

Arabia headed into the kitchen. As she passed through the entry, she pushed apart the beaded curtain and ducked her head. The swinging strands collided, creating a musical clatter that appealed to her avian aesthetics. In the same vein, she loved how the multi-colored glass sparkled with all the colors of flame when they caught the firelight.

She made a beeline for the cabinet where she stored her alcohol. She had just a few bottles: a good white wine, an even finer red, and inexpensive versions of both she used for cooking. She shoved all aside, however, and reached for the carafe at the far back. With due care, she grasped the neck of the crystal vessel and lifted it out. The rich burgundy trapped the light and kept it suspended so it glowed with the incandescence of the darkest grade of amber. Mesmerized, Arabia gazed into its depths and sank her teeth into her lower lip. Despite the enormous amount of preparation she'd put into tonight, she couldn't shake the icy grip of uncertainty. Like an undead thing, doubt had its talons embedded in her gut.

"Damn it, Chase," she whispered. "Why are you so damn stubborn?"

Chase called from the front room. "What was that?"

Arabia gave a guilty start. The abrupt motion jolted the burgundy so it swished about inside the decanter like a tiny sea in a storm, crashing up against the crystal sides. Although she strove to justify what she was about to do, a vicious sliver of guilt remained deeply embedded in her heart. She didn't want to resort to enchantment to settle the matter of Chase's attraction to her. The stubborn man, with his ridiculous sense of honor and absurd hang-ups, left her no other choice, though.

"Nothing!" she called out, shoving the cabinet doors closed with a loud clang. She decided to initiate some small talk to buy herself time. "So, Reidar's in Australia, huh?"

After a pause, Chase replied, "Yeah, on business."

"You already said that. What sort of business?" Arabia placed the decanter upon the altar she kept in the corner of the kitchen beside the wood-burning stove. Swiftly, she struck a long match and held the flame to the wicks of the red candles. She placed two wine glasses side by side on the dais and selected a small vial, which she held to eye level for inspection.

Ceridwen's tears: shimmering liquid gold.

The precious drops had been a gift from the Celtic goddess of magic and were essential component of the Heart's Desire spell. The enchantment wouldn't work without them.

"I'm afraid I can't say." Chase employed that neutral tone she found so infuriating.

"You mean you won't. You're Reidar's best friend *and* his attorney, but I'm supposed to believe you don't know why he's on another continent?"

Chase chuckled. "He's in negotiations with a multi-national corporation to purchase land rights for an endangered species preserve."

She harrumphed to convey her disapproval. "That's my big brother: champion of the earth. Strangers matter more to him than his own family."

"That's unfair." Predictably, Chase launched into a sound, well-reasoned, and lengthy defense of Reidar's business practices. Naturally, his arguments were terribly convincing... and she'd heard it all a hundred times before.

Arabia smiled, because she'd bought herself the

much-needed time, and threw out the occasional comment. She repeatedly challenged Chase on points of logic, being deliberately contrary, which served to get him going all over again.

While they talked, she added a pinch of crushed flower petals to the burgundy: red rose for love, orange lily for passion, and gold protea for change and transformation. Lastly, she uncorked the vial of Ceridwen's tears and filled an eyedropper. She held the tip over the opening of the vessel and allowed three drops to fall.

Arabia held the decanter to eye level and swirled the contents to mix everything together. A whorl of anxiety whirled in her gut. Goddess, but she was nervous! She shouldn't be. The true power of the spell derived from the divine essence of the goddess. Three drops were more than plenty. Still, she worried. Chase was the most mule headed man she'd ever met. He gave stubborn a whole new meaning. What if three droplets weren't sufficient to overcome his formidable defenses? The man had more excuses than a politician in a sex scandal for why they shouldn't be together. If anyone could resist the Heart's Desire spell, it was Chase Baron.

Arabia, teetering on the edge of indecision, then tipped over.

"Just a few more..." She added three more golden beads but hesitated. Three and nine were both significant figures. Six, not so much. So, for the sake of the numbers, she opted to infuse three more droplets, bringing the total to nine. If that didn't do it, nothing would.

Time to throw the dice and see how they landed.

In the front room, Chase's foot thumped on the floorboards. In a voice sharp with suspicion, he asked, "Arabia, what's taking so long?"

"Nothing! I just need to rinse out the wine glasses. Give me a sec." She leaned and whacked the faucet so water ran into the sink.

In a hushed whisper, she chanted the words to the ritual.

> "Pray, hear my words, Ceridwen,
> Mother of Magic,
> Goddess who is Wise.
> Upon this full moon dark, this season
> of ice,
> When the mists between the worlds
> are thin,
> I call upon your power to arise and
> come to me.

Heart's desire called forth.
Ceridwen, assess my worth.
Freedom from slavery, naked in
    your rites.
Liberated from fear and doubt
    this night.
Before the dawn, deliver my heart's
    delight and desire.
Love is the law unto all beings.
My will be done, so mote it be."

CHAPTER 7

WOLF GONE FERAL

November 7th...

When she incanted the last word of the spell, fairy-tale sparkles shimmered across the surface of the wine. A streak of red and gold rose in a ribbon of pure magic. The glass warmed and the most amazing scent wafted into the air.

Arabia lifted the decanter to her face. She closed her eyes and drank in the wondrous aroma. An incredible rush of energy surged through her. It tingled along her nerve endings. She felt as though she was floating—and that was coming from a woman who *literally* knew what it meant to fly.

Yes, *this* was right. The spell had worked.

Ever so carefully, she lifted the decanter and filled both glasses midway. By the time she finished pouring and turned off the water, the glimmer faded, the burgundy restored to its normal color.

Showtime.

A glass in each hand, she passed through the curtain of glass beads into the front room. Chase stood before the fireplace. When she entered, he turned to face her. His gaze held something intense and terrifying that sent shivers coursing through her body. He parted his lips as if to speak but said nothing.

It didn't matter. She had plenty on her mind she needed to share. To get started, she took a deep breath. "So, Chase..."

"So," he drawled in that here-it-comes tone. It ruffled her feathers for sure, and it irritated her to no end how easily he got to her.

"Right now, you're wondering why we're not talking about what just happened between us. You've already speculated on the dozen different things I might say and prepared a rebuttal for each one."

Chase grinned. "Rebuttals, huh?"

"Rebuttals," she said firmly. "I know exactly what's going on in that complicated head of yours."

Arabia drifted closer, swishing her hips. With predatory intent, he tracked the motion. When she arched the small of her back, lifting her breasts, he stared. Some women might've found his blatant interest offensive, but not Arabia. She loved it. It meant he'd noticed her as a woman... *at last.* His helpless fascination granted her a visceral rush of satisfaction.

"So you're a mind reader now?" Chase narrowed his eyes and brought his gaze to her face.

She smirked. "No. It's not that hard to understand what a man is thinking about right after he gets done kissing you. I totally rocked your world, but you don't want to confess how deeply I affect you. Your thoughts are crowded with all the usual excuses: I'm your best friend's baby sister. You're eight years older than me, so it's cradle robbing."

"You talk like you know me."

"I do know you. Too well. You're a good man, an ethical and honorable man, and your moral compass interferes with what would be right for you." She raised her hand, offering him a wine glass, and rocked it just a bit so the burgundy rolled like a crimson sea.

Chase growled deep in his throat. "Stop. I'm not playing your game."

She threw back her head, tossing her hair, and laughed. "Big B, this isn't a game. It's life and death."

He raised his brow. "You mean life *or* death...?"

"No, I don't mean any such thing. You'd understand if you'd paid any attention at all to the fate-spinning chants my people sing."

"You know I'm tone deaf. Music doesn't mean anything to me."

"You don't have to feel the rhythm to grasp the fundamental concept of fate spinning," Arabia said in a tone thin with impatience. She didn't believe him either when he claimed to not understand. The Baron Pack and the Silverwind Conspiracy—wolves and ravens—had been allied for centuries. No wolf of the tribe could be as ignorant of ravenborn magic as Chase claimed to be, especially not the alpha.

Arabia stepped close, lifting the glass so the rim was just below his mouth in an act of considered temptation. Artful seduction. She'd done her research. Beverly Hills werewolf: The expensive burgundy should suit Chase's refined tastes to a T. To be sure, she swirled it so the rich aroma would lift to fill his nostrils.

Grim-faced, he glanced down, and she held her breath while he raised his hand, then paused. She struggled to stay still, but the effort cost her dearly. For the spell to work, they needed to drink together. She wondered what the odds were that he'd join her in a toast. Probably not very good, given her track record and how well he knew her.

"Arabia, what's this about?" Chase lifted his golden gaze to her face. He penetrated her soul, yet that couldn't be true. If he saw her, truly saw her, he wouldn't have to ask that ridiculous question.

Caught on a hook—the force of his will—she teetered on the verge of confession. It'd be so much easier to tell him the truth: an open, candid statement of her doubts and desires. Then she remembered... *Oh yeah, she'd tried honesty—that kiss.* And stubborn, principled Chase Baron had rejected her advances, once again regulating her to the status of a girl incapable of knowing her own mind. So she opened her mouth to offer the standard evasions, and it occurred to her—there could be no better defense than the truth. Later, when he accused her of misbehaving, she would remind him that she'd been honest. He, of course, would refuse to believe, but she could hardly be blamed for *that*, too.

Could she?

"You were right. I set the whole thing up just to get you to come to Stillwater. It's all part of a complicated scheme designed to get you into my bed. Here, I hope you like burgundy." Arabia thrust the glass toward him again, making a concentrated effort to stay steady. Her arms trembled, though, and the wine rippled, betraying her nervousness.

Reflexively, Chase took the glass. Lips parted, he stared at her in blank astonishment. To her horror, she thought she perceived hurt on his face, not what she'd intended at all. The bright shininess vanished after an instant, fast enough to convince her that she must've imagined it.

"Hilarious," he said with sour-lime sarcasm.

"Yeah, I'm a riot." She smiled, but her stomach gurgled with acidity. Her humiliation knew no depths. What a nightmare! The man she loved assumed her interest in him was a joke. Just about the only thing worse he could've done would've been to actually take her seriously and laugh.

"Arabia..." Chase said in that tone he used prior to a lecture.

"Here's mud in your eye." Arabia lifted her cup in a toast. Her pulse kicked into overtime, and her nerves jangled like bells.

"Cheers." Chase raised his glass, then he hesitated.

Her breath caught in her throat. If he refused to drink with her, the love spell would fizzle. Put poetically, the moment of reckoning was upon them. The magic would free Chase of all his doubts and inhibitions, enabling him to perceive his heart's desire. It remained to be seen whether he longed for *her* or some other woman.

Courage failed her. Arabia couldn't stand it any longer, so she closed her eyes and downed it all at once. Wine overflowed the corners of her mouth, spilling along her throat. The fine burgundy had an exceptional bouquet, a refined airiness that unfurled to reveal subtle notes of cherry and smoke. Unfortunately, she couldn't bring herself to savor it, so she chugged the last drop.

As the spell took hold, euphoria ignited a spark in her core. It grew to a flame, radiating through her torso, and spread to her limbs, which turned syrupy. In her heart, her mind, and her soul, she'd never harbored any real doubt, but the spell delivered the gold stamp. Chase Baron always had been—and always would be—the light of her life.

Her heart's desire.

She popped her eyes open, gasping on an indrawn breath in time to watch Chase sip his wine. He lowered his glass and swiped his tongue across his sensuous lips, catching the last bit of the burgundy. Transfixed, she tracked the alluring gesture, hungering for the firm press of his mouth and the taste of him. She especially admired the way his form-fitting clothing clung to every plane and curve of his chiseled physique.

A wolf in fine wool. How many levels of wrong? She couldn't count.

Chase snarled low in his throat. The primitive rumble reduced her to shaking in her lace-up knee-high boots. Adrenaline surged through her. She jerked and took a step back, lifting her arms in a reflexive impulse to assume her raven form. Escape counted as the last thing on her list of priorities, though. She quelled her instinct for flight and lowered her arms, but not before Chase noticed.

"Are you afraid of me?" Chase's voice had a dulcet timbre one hundred percent different from his usual tenor.

"No. Should I be?" She wasn't lying. Contrary to the core, danger thrilled her.

Chase drifted closer, stalking her with a hunter's intent. With a swift motion, he plucked the wine glass from her fingers, then set it and his own on the bookcase. "Should you be?"

"That's what I just asked you." Arabia retreated just so he could pursue her. She thrummed with anticipation, reveling in being the target of his focus. *Finally,* after so many years of unrequited attraction. For the first time in her entire life, she believed he saw her and perceived a mature woman with real, wanton desires.

He frowned. "I don't know. I feel... strange."

"Strange how? Good? Bad?" Arabia asked, more than a little anxious. The spell didn't negate his ability to reason or resist its effects. She worried his formidable intellect would allow him to figure out what'd happened before they resolved how he felt.

"Good. Very good." He looked straight at her and smiled. She perceived the difference then. At the moment, his wolf dominated his psyche.

She shivered and her stomach dropped. She sped her retreat, but thanks to the tiny dimensions of her front room, they wound up traveling in a tight circle around the table. No matter how fast she moved, he stayed three steps behind her. "I think maybe I should be scared."

"You should be." He sounded sadistically pleased with the prospect. A wolf gone feral, hunger glittered in his golden eyes.

"Well, I'm not." Arabia jutted her chin out in defiance and took a careless step. Her back hit the wall. Nowhere left to run. Like a guest late to the party, common sense whispered in the back of her brain, and fear tickled her nerve endings. What had she been thinking? A silly raven was no match for a werewolf. With eyes like platters, she tilted her head back and stared up at him.

"Good." Chase loomed over her, bigger and badder than life. His distinctive scent wafted about her; the musky mark of a predator. He grinned, showing off big, ultra-white teeth. All that much better to eat her with?

Goddess, please let it be so.

CHAPTER 8

BIG AND BAD

November 7th...

Arabia caught hold of the lapels of Chase's suit coat. She spread her legs wide and arched her hips toward him in an open invitation. Her four-inch heels gave her that extra bit of boost necessary for her to connect. Her belly bumped against the swollen bulge in his crotch. She moaned and he groaned, echoing her intense need.

"Chase." She rubbed herself against his groin with the intention of teasing him. It backfired and damn near drove her mad.

"Arabia." A low growl rumbled in his throat, and the muskiness of his scent intensified. Chase caught the sides of her face and bent his dark head. He crushed her lips beneath his own and shoved her against the wall. He pressed his chest against her, crushing her breasts flat, and her nipples hardened to tight pebbles at the tantalizing friction.

Chase licked her upper lip, a swift tease, coaxing her to yield to him. The moment Arabia parted her lips, he slipped his tongue past her guard. He stroked the smoothness of her teeth and then delved deeper, emulating the primal act of mating. He tasted like enchantment—rich burgundy and dark chocolate. Delicious sin. Voracious, he feasted on her as a starving man at a sumptuous feast. She shivered, caught in a rhapsody of alarm and arousal. An inkling of fear lingered that he'd consume her whole, but she longed for it, too. Urgency gripped her, an acute ache that bordered on physical pain.

The kiss went on forever. Dizziness swept over her. Breathless, she clung to him for support and dug her nails into the solid wall of his chest. Chase read her like a book. He broke the embrace and they both gasped. Head spinning, Arabia blinked. Fog filled her mind. Her gaze locked on the prominent swell of his Adam's apple, which undulated as his throat worked.

"Am I going too fast?" Chase asked, panting.

"Not fast enough." As a pointed hint, she tugged at his suit coat with fumbling fingers.

"Impatient, aren't you?" Chase chuckled and shed his suit coat and his blue dress shirt. He took his sweet time about undressing, which irked her to no end, but her minor irritation fled as fabric parted.

Male perfection—his bronzed skin covered robust muscles. Sculpted lines defined him: the curve of his strong shoulders and the sleek stroke that divided his defined pecs. His nipples were flat discs nested in the dusting of dark hair covering the solid wall of his chest. A study in symmetry, he had ripped, six-pack abs, and the chiseled grooves of his pelvic girdle were sharp enough to cut glass. His Adonis belt disappeared beneath the waistband of his trim black pants, a devil's fast track to wicked temptation.

She feasted on him with her eyes, devouring every glorious inch. He rotated to toss his clothing at the coat rack, scoring a neat catch on one of the hooks. When he turned back, he caught her staring in rapt fascination.

"Take your time to marvel, baby." He flashed a wolfish smile and trailed his fingers across his chest, a la strip tease. The man had the body and the moves to perform as an exotic dancer if he ever decided to give up the law.

"Aren't you a cocky bastard?" She infused her

tone with disdain and narrowed her eyes. "I'm starting to wonder if you're more rooster than wolf."

"I'm a wolf, you silly bird." He grinned, signaling his acceptance of her challenge. Let the bantering commence...

"Yeah? Get your big bad ass over here and prove it."

Chase released a ferocious growl that built in the depths of his chest and rolled from his throat. It came in startling contrast to the loud tearing of fabric. The mother of pearl buttons from her ruined blouse struck the floor with bright pings like raindrops. He jerked the fabric away, and a blast of cool air washed over her skin.

Arabia yelped and then laughed, reckless with delight. Beneath the top, she wore a black corset that laced in front. She adored corsets, the constriction of being bound. It pushed her bosom high and tight, so much so her nipples threatened to burst free. The tattoo of a vine covered in delicate indigo flowers began at the base of her throat and twined between her breasts.

"You're so beautiful, Arabia," Chase said, hushed and reverent. The weight of his gaze caressed her.

"Am I?" Arabia asked in a small voice. She hated

how much self-doubt the question betrayed, exposing her deepest insecurity.

"Beyond description," Chase said with effusive conviction that filled her with joy. When he seized the corset's laces, she arched her chest. Comically, the deft Chase Baron actually fumbled with the bow.

"Let me." She giggled and swept his hands aside, undoing the bow with an expert tug. From there, she made swift work of it, loosening the top laces. The stiff sides of the corset parted, revealing her breasts. Arabia groaned in pure pleasure, achieving a rapturous bodicegasm.

"Feels that good, eh?" Chase's grin widened.

"You've no idea," Arabia said, blushing to her toes. It took an act of will not to squirm beneath his avid gaze.

"I didn't know you had piercings." He stroked her curves and agitated her sensitive buds with quick swipes of his thumbs. More gently, he touched the heart-shaped end of the gold posts that pierced her peaks.

"Only since I was fourteen," Arabia panted, struggling to remain coherent. It wound up being an absolute impossibility. The intense heat and firmness of his hands covering her breasts destroyed all rational thought.

"Kinky. I approve." Chase snickered and feathered his fingers over the taut ribs of the corset. "I'm going to leave this on."

"Oh? Why?" She loved the wantonness of her cleavage spilling free while her ribcage remained bound. She suspected he did, too, but she wanted to hear him say it.

"Because you look so damn sexy, my cock hurts. I want to fuck these beauties." He cupped her breasts and tugged on the posts through her nipples again.

"Oh. Please! Harder," Arabia moaned and arched against him, begging for further punishment.

"So you like it rough?" Chase worked her flesh with the skill of a sculptor, crafting a masterpiece of pleasure. He lowered his mouth to her bosom and laved his tongue over her nipple. At an unhurried pace, he stroked the gold hearts on the post of her piercing, alternating side to side.

"I love rough." Arabia threaded her fingers through his short, dark hair. The glossy locks slid like silk through her grip.

"Hold on tight," he warned in a voice rich with sinful promise that sent shivers down her spine. Her heart fluttered like wings in flight, and she got slippery between the thighs.

A whimper of purest anticipation escaped her.

Arabia closed her eyes and clutched at his shoulders —a good thing, too. Chase treated her as his own personal playground. He slathered loving attention on her breasts, neglected not a square inch, and conducted adventuresome forays along other paths. He suckled her throat, nipped her earlobe, and nuzzled the inside of her elbow and wrist.

Arabia fell into a helpless trance. She endured the torment of his mouth and hands as an eager martyr—a willing sacrifice made to him. He tortured her with pleasure, lifted her into rapture, and plunged her into an ecstasy of despair. She existed for his kisses and his caresses. In every way that mattered, she belonged to him—his woman, his pet, his lover. However he wanted, whatever he required her to be.

Teeth-rattling tremors shook her. Intense heat engulfed her. The room must have been on fire, but when she forced open her eyes, no flames surrounded her. Her eyelids drooped and shut once again under the weight of pleasurable lethargy, but the reprieve didn't last long.

"Chase!" Arabia muttered his name as a weak protest when the ravishment ceased suddenly and without warning. She stole a curious peek through her eyelashes.

He sank to his knees and raised the hem of her plaid micro-mini skirt, exposing her to his heated gaze. The skimpy fabric of her underwear provided a thin veil of protection that was soon gone. With a hungry growl, he tugged her panties to mid-thigh. Arabia squeaked and bucked, but he pinned her. No escaping the big, bad wolf. My, what trouble she'd gotten herself into!

"So tasty. A feast fit for an alpha." His breath huffed and puffed hot across her skin. He flicked the tip of his tongue across the lips of her pussy. Sweet agony.

"Chase, please! Stop teasing!" She squirmed, dying of want and need.

"Who's teasing?" Chase asked with a sultry chuckle. He caught her slim thighs in his large hands, immobilized her legs, and then spread her. His lower face fit into the V of her thighs as though she'd been made to order for him. He drove his tongue into her folds, delving for the pearl buried at the apex. When he found the treasure, he strummed her until she screamed.

Pretty pleases and pleas for mercy rained from her lips but fell on deaf ears. Chase lapped at her pussy, pushing her soft flesh every which way. He employed coarse, powerful strokes. A vague recollection flitted through the back of her mind. Something she'd once heard about the tongue being the strongest muscle in the body. As he pushed into her core, she became convinced it must be true. If anything, the man must engage in power lifting! In the Tongue Olympics, he'd take the gold medal for brute strength. Then he performed a wild, twisty gymnastics maneuver about her clit that left her eyes crossed, and she awarded him a medal for dexterity.

"Chase, please." In a fit of frustrated arousal, she sank her nails into his shoulders, drawing drops of blood that mingled with the sweat on his skin. The scratches healed almost immediately.

He chuckled. "I always suspected a good, hard fuck would make you pliable, Arabia. I had no idea how effective it'd be."

"You bastard," she spat, and he laughed.

"Such a pretty mouth. I'd love to fill it with my cock." Chase rose but kept her imprisoned within the cage of his arms. Her creamy cum glistened on his mustache and beard.

"I dare you." She bared her teeth.

"Later." The gleam in his gaze made it a promise. When he kissed her, she tasted her salty-sweetness on his mouth.

She nipped him, drawing a trickle of blood. The

caress of his lips hardened, and the kiss turned punishing. He lifted her skirt and cupped her mound. Too gently, he eased a single digit into her cleft, withdrawing and entering her with maddeningly soft strokes. A sweet promise but not nearly enough.

Chase pushed a second finger into her slick channel. Arabia gasped, and the powerful walls of her vagina contracted. A moan built in her chest. Better, so much better, but still not enough. She arched toward him, begging for more.

Arabia reached for his belt buckle but the contrary contraption defied her clumsy attempts to open it. Finally, she loosened it, but before she could tear open his fly, he blocked her hands. Like a child denied candy, she cried out.

When their kiss broke, she gasped and demanded. "Take me."

"Patience. You can wait." He withdrew his paired fingers and penetrated her with his middle digit, literally giving her the bird. The inane thought set her to giggling, and she wondered if the pun had occurred to him. Three hours ago, she'd have sworn the staid attorney was incapable of appreciating dirty humor, but now she wasn't so sure.

"I've been patient for years. What am I waiting

for?" She rolled her hips toward him, begging for more.

"I have to be sure you're ready. I don't want to hurt you," Chase said, dead serious in his delivery.

"My, aren't we cocky?" Arabia grinned, certain the man must be exaggerating his size. Guys liked to do that. But when he failed to wink or crack a smile, her smugness faltered.

"In a word—yes." He finished what she'd started and opened his fly. He shoved his pants and boxers down and flattened her against the wall too fast for her to get a good look at his manhood.

A thick rod bashed against her corset, but the ribbed garment kept the wolf at bay. A startled hiccup interrupted Arabia's thoughts. Good goddess! That thing couldn't possibly be as big as it seemed... could it? She cast a hasty glance down, but Chase had already wrapped his hands about her waist. He lifted her high and pinioned her back to the wall. The bulbous head of his cock nudged at her glossy folds, but the bunched material of her skirt hid him from view. If curiosity killed ravens as well as it slayed cats, she was one dead corvid.

Arabia crossed her ankles at the small of Chase's back, grateful for the added support her boots provided. Bunched muscles stood out beneath his sweat-slickened skin. Tension thrummed through his entire body as he seated his crown against her entrance. He remained rigid, holding his strength in check.

Arabia trembled, fully expecting him to plunge in, and it was a measure of his self-control when he nudged into her. True to his word, he didn't leave so much as a bruise on her skin.

Even though he'd already prepared her with his fingers, her body resisted his advance. Amazement rounded her eyes even as he stretched her wider than she thought she could bear, and then a touch more after that.

"You win," she whimpered. "I shouldn't have laughed."

"Laugh all you like, my sweet raven. I'll always have the last laugh."

He impaled her.

Arabia wailed so high she strained her vocal chords. His engorged shaft, as stiff as steel rebar, filled her to bursting. So thick, it felt like he'd cleaved her into two halves. The blunt tip battered against the entrance to her womb; his balls smashed against her. Despite the countless hours she'd spent with her fingers crammed into her sex, fantasizing about this exact moment, the reality exceeded her wildest imaginings. Her lady parts had never been more impressed.

"Are you okay?" Chase peered into her eyes, his face set in a stony mask. He suffered from the intensity of his restraint; it hurt to witness.

"Perfect," Arabia all but moaned. She opened and closed her grip on his hips, unconsciously mirroring the contractions of her core about his cock.

"Are you sure?" Still, he held back.

"Stop being such a lawyer." She beamed, intending to offer confident reassurance, but she feared her smile turned into a feral grimace. Fine, she'd let her body do her talking for her. Cinching her legs, she applied the heel of her boot to his backside. "Giddy up."

Chase laughed from the belly, but with difficulty. An odd rigorousness muffled the sound, and it saddened her to observe his struggle. Her poor, beloved, stuffy wolf. He needed her every bit as much as she needed him.

"What a mule-headed mount you are. I wish I'd worn spurs," Arabia grumbled, and tapped his ass again. "Fuck me harder."

"Fine, you asked for it." Chase withdrew and returned with a powerful thrust. The motion wrung a cry of pure torment from Arabia. When he repeated the motion, he penetrated so deep that his pubic bone rubbed deliciously over her clit. Starbursts of pleasure exploded behind her eyes. She yelped and clung to him.

Rode him.

They caught fire together, a feverish passion that burned out of control. It consumed rational thought, and stripped them down to their primal nature. As merciless as a wolf on the hunt, Chase drove into her at a brutal pace. But ravens had always been partners to wolves, never prey. Arabia rose to the challenge and matched him stroke for stroke, giving as good as she got.

Ravenborn had not the equivalent to a mating bite, but Arabia understood wolf-shifter custom well. She pressed her mouth to his shoulder and sank her teeth. When she broke skin, he jerked and snarled. The hot, coppery tang of blood hit her tongue and she drank while deliberately turning her head to the side, offering him her throat. An intense pang of disappointment crashed over her when Chase didn't claim her in return. She dismissed it, assuring herself it wasn't a rejection. Chase wasn't the sort to make a lifetime commitment in the heat of passion. Tonight's evening of spontaneous, wholly unplanned passion might very well be enough to put the poor man in therapy. A quirky smirk played on her lips. Then the tsunami of their union crashed over her, drowning reason.

Arabia's climax blindsided her. Without warning, she spiraled into a crazy whirl. Her entire body clenched—an explosion centered in her core. A white-hot blaze of suns gone nova enveloped her. She tilted back her head and thrilled her quintessential joy to the heavens.

Chase pursued her into ecstasy. He stiffened. Deep within her, his cock underwent a series of sharp tugs as he spilled his hot seed. Throwing back his head, he loosened a long, loud howl into the night.

CHAPTER 9

December 9th...

Chase leaned against the doorjamb of the Stillwater Correctional facility. His body was present but his mind? A million miles away, submersed in sensual recollection of his tryst with Arabia. Her scent filled his nostrils; her taste lingered on his tongue. It'd been like that a lot lately, ever since the evening of the spell when he'd made love with her for hours on end.

Chase had never experienced a pinnacle of carnal delight to rival the one he'd shared with Arabia *that night*. All. Night. Long. He wasn't a sexual novice—not by a long shot—but with each recounting, his recollection of how amazing it had been expanded to the point where he wouldn't have believed it was real. Except he'd been there... and he was obsessed.

Awake or asleep—it didn't matter—daydreams and wet dreams plagued him. And those memories kept him going. He got hot and horny, and always in the worst possible circumstances: painful erections straining against his tight suit trousers in the middle of court. He sweated and swore, wondering if his ravenborn princess had driven him thoroughly *and* irrevocably mad.

Spellbound.

Husky female laughter punctured his reverie. "She must be one amazing witchy-woman."

Chase jerked his thoughts out of the fantasy and snapped his head around. He ended up face to face with a statuesque woman as tall as him. She had platinum blonde hair and striking features, and piercing blue eyes that looked straight through him.

"Excuse me? Do I know you?" Chase tried for a flinty stare meant to intimidate.

"Not directly." The blonde didn't blink, but she did smile, and it was smug, superior, and all-knowing.

He hesitated. Chase didn't recognize her, and she didn't look like a ravenborn to him, but that didn't mean much when referencing people renowned for artifice and legerdemain. Paranoia needled him. Had she read his mind? Maybe he'd misheard. But c'mon—a witchy-woman? It had to be an allusion to Arabia.

The blonde tipped her chin. "Whoever put that huge smile on your face... She must be an amazing woman."

He frowned, unsure of how to respond. Without understanding the full how or why of it, he mumbled, "She is amazing."

The strange woman pushed past him and was lost to view. Chase considered pursuing her and demanding answers, but there were too many witnesses, and she hadn't actually done anything worthy of a confrontation. Better to let it go. The entrance had too much traffic for his taste, so he relocated a yard to the right and planted a mental flag, designating the ten-foot parcel as his property.

This was temporary Baron Pack territory.

This spot.

Right here.

The borders stretched from the entrance to his right and the potted palm on the left. While it might not qualify as a legal claim, he had squatting rights. And to prove it, he crossed his arms over his chest, braced his back against the wall, and dared anyone to try and take it from him. For the most part, it worked. Members of the milling crowd cast sharp glances in his direction but otherwise gave him a wide birth. Unfortunately, it did nothing to dim the racket.

A conspiracy of ravens...

Chase had always considered the phrase to be a complete oxymoron. Conspiracy conjured images of cloak and dagger collusion, hushed conversations in dark and dangerous alleyways conducted by spies clad in high-collared black trench coats. In actuality, a gathering of raven-shifters was the exact opposite of quiet. Aside from the guards and Chase, every other occupant of the visitor's center was ravenborn. The entire Silverwind Conspiracy had turned out in force to show support for their jailed princess. Every last bird in the bunch was talking—*loudly*—over each other.

At the center of the congregation, Evelyn Jensen, the Silverwind Queen, held court with her husband, Tobias, and Arabia. The rest of the conspiracy gathered about the royal family in a defensive ring. Chase recognized about half of those present, which said a lot, given the long-standing friendship between the Silverwind Conspiracy and the Baron Pack.

Chase's inner wolf plastered his ears against his skull, tipped back his head, and *brayed* in misery.

"Whoa, who rained on your parade, Mr. Werewolf?" a woman asked in a voice both light and mocking, and hauntingly similar to Arabia.

"Hello, Branwen." Chase turned his face a notch, addressing Arabia's fraternal twin sister. He kept his guard up, unsure of what reception to expect.

"Hello? Is that the best you can do?" Branwen tossed her long, dark hair and opened her arms in a silent demand. Her eyes were a striking shade of jade.

"It's good to see you." A smile cracked his face, and he swooped and gathered her into a brotherly hug. While the twins were the same height, Arabia had about ten pounds on her sister. Ten *good* pounds that enhanced her earthy curves, whereas Branwen felt as straight and light as a twig in his arms... And what the hell was he thinking, comparing the two women? Growing up, his attitude toward Branwen and Arabia had been familial, equal parts annoyance and affection. It pricked his conscience to admit that his feelings for Arabia no longer resembled anything even remotely platonic.

Chase grimaced and pulled away from Branwen a little too fast. She knit her brow and bestowed a funny look on him. Questioning his sanity? No, Branwen was far too self-satisfied and amused for his tastes. Thankfully, she didn't call him out on the source of his embarrassment.

"It's good to see you, too." Branwen stepped back, giving him space, just not ten feet of it, coming to stand beside the potted palm. He had to turn to face her, putting his back to the door. *Crafty woman.* With one deft maneuver, she'd forced him to surrender the defensive position he'd assumed.

"It's been a while."

"Almost a year." She nodded encouragement. "How've you been?"

Chase hesitated before answering. The truth? He'd been working long hours on Arabia's defense. He was tired and grumpy. He missed his home and his pack, and he secretly feared the case was unwinnable. None of which Branwen needed to hear.

"Good," he said, "and you?"

"I joined an indie rock band," Branwen said and flashed a Mona Lisa smile. A woman with a secret.

"Really?" Chase wasn't surprised. Branwen was into music, more so than Arabia. The twins had taken piano lessons as kids. He recalled Branwen banging away on the keyboard, practicing, years after Arabia had given up.

"Really. It's also a coyote band."

"That sounds...interesting." Chase *felt* his upper lip curling. Coyotes—he didn't like coyotes. Sly, shifty bastards to the last. Not to be trusted.

"Isn't it cool?" Branwen watched him like a hawk. (See what he did there?) Her eyes shone bright and avid. An immediate sign she was baiting him.

"It is. Cool." He spoke through his teeth.

"It's not an all-coyote band. We have a werewolf in our band, too. He's our roadie."

"You do?" His stomach soured on the thought of a werewolf desperate enough to sink to joining a coyote band. WTF? What was wrong with the poor bastard?

"Yup, we do." Branwen sucked in her cheeks. Oh boy. She wanted him to screw up.

"It's good to hear."

"Oh, and we have a cranky Kodiak mama bear-shifter."

"Part of the Romanoff Clan?" He grew keen with interest. Now, Kodiaks were a rare and long-lived breed who exerted extensive influence in SoCal. It struck him as unlikely that one would ally herself with a hodgepodge coyote band.

"No idea." Branwen shrugged. If the brat had been chewing gum, she'd have popped a bubble.

Okay, moving on.

"So, you play keyboard for this band."

"Yup." She furrowed her forehead. No doubt annoyed over his clever evasion of her trickery.

"Interesting." He strove to remain neutral and mentally patted himself on the back for doing a good job thus far.

"I've chosen the leader of the band as my mate." She smiled blithely, daring him to say something.

Don't ask... don't ask... don't ask. Chase tied his tongue into knots with the effort it took to keep quiet. He only managed because it'd be a huge mistake. He already had his hands full dealing with the convoluted concerns and myriad mysteries of one ravenborn woman. He didn't need more.

His knobby tongue lodged in his throat, cutting off his air.

"Chase, are you okay?" Branwen brought her hands up in apparent concern.

"Congratulations!" Chase forced out. He twisted his mouth into a parody of a smile.

"Disco doesn't know he's my mate yet. At least, he hasn't realized it."

"Disco?"

"Disco Cordova." She bobbed her head.

"He sounds like a Mexican Tiki bar." A vein throbbed in his temple.

She narrowed her eyes. "You have something against Tiki bars?"

"Hell, no. I love rum. Do you need me to beat some sense into this asshole who's dissing you?"

"What? No! Don't be such an asshole. Disco is a great guy. He's hella good-looking. And ripped. He has a voice like John Lennon, and when he dances, it's like John Travolta's second coming."

"John Travolta isn't dead."

"He's not?" Her eyes glazed.

"Nope. At least, not the last time I checked."

Branwen scowled in vexation.

"Why is this guy ignoring you?" Chase flexed his hands. He considered Branwen his little sister. She obviously had a thing for this Disco jerkoff, but it sounded like the coyote needed to have some sense beat into him.

"It's complicated." Branwen teared up and bit her lip. She shook her head, sending her hair flying. "Please, drop it. I can manage Disco. He's just... mule-headed."

Chase cleared his tight throat. "Hopefully, the kids will inherit your brains."

"I wish the same for you." Branwen directed an irritated glance at her sister but gave no clue as to why.

Kids? Wait. What? Did she mean his kids with Arabia? Oh shit! Panic-shaped energy surged through Chase. Did Branwen know something he didn't? He and Arabia had only shared one night together, but he hadn't worn protection.

Branwen arched her brow expectantly.

Chase tripped over his own tongue. "Uh, thanks."

They stared at each other while time skipped along.

Eventually, Branwen asked, "So, why are you hiding over here in the corner?"

"I didn't want to intrude on your family reunion. I also wasn't sure I was welcome." Chase turned his head, staring across the range of ravenborn.

Chase wanted nothing more than to go over and join Arabia. He longed to go to his lover and wrap his arm around her shoulders. However, he couldn't shake the feeling of being an intruder at her family gathering. The odd wolf out, so to speak. Only a fool could've missed the quick glances stolen in his direction and the hushed exchanges behind raised hands. It gave him an inkling of how many people were gossiping about him and Arabia.

"Don't be silly. No one is upset with you for sleeping with my sister. Gods, this is the twenty-first century." She rolled her eyes.

"Does the whole conspiracy know?" He stifled a groan. Suspicions confirmed.

"Of course we do! Our heir-apparent is having an affair with the alpha of the Baron Pack? It's all anyone is talking about."

"What about Reidar?" Chase clenched his jaws. Damn it. He should've trusted his instincts, reached out to his best friend, and gotten ahead of this thing. Instead, he'd used Reidar's extended business trip to Australia as an excuse for delaying.

"Of course. My parents had a conference call with Reidar yesterday to bring him up to speed on the good news. My brother is flying back to the states today." Branwen opened her mouth, but something beyond Chase snagged her attention.

Someone.

A soft footfall came from behind Chase and a man's hand caught his arm. Chase braced for a fight. Then he caught Reidar Jensen's familiar scent. Some of the tension bled from the werewolf's shoulders. Time to pay the piper... Chase performed an about-face to confront his blood brother.

"We need to talk," Reidar Jensen said in a stern

voice, full of flint and steel. Fiery sparks glinted in his onyx eyes...with the promise of flame. Obvious tension thrummed through his long, lithe body.

"You don't say," Chase drawled.

"Hello to you, too, big brother." Boldly, Branwen waltzed between the two men and threw her arms around Reidar's neck. She planted a kiss square on his cheek.

"Hi, Branwen." Reidar embraced his sister, but he stared over the top of her head at Chase. His gaze never wavered.

Chase returned his friend's regard. Reidar hadn't knifed him in the back, but that didn't mean they weren't headed for a fight. After all, Chase *had* slept with the man's little sister. Just the thought sent the sting of guilt through him even though it was perfectly irrational. Arabia hadn't been a virgin, and this was the modern era. His conscience, though, didn't give a fuck about pragmatism.

"Okay, I'll leave you boys to hash it out." Branwen flitted off.

"Do you want to talk here?" Chase asked.

"Outside," Reidar clipped. Without waiting for an answer, he strode toward the entrance. Chase would've taken offense over being ordered about—

and the assumption he'd obey—by anyone else. Reidar, though, was entitled to his anger.

Tightlipped, Chase followed his best friend into the parking lot. The two men crossed the pavement in grim silence and came to stand on a snowy knoll beneath tall pine trees cloaked in white.

The atmosphere crackled. They squared off. Reidar settled into a brawler's stance with his fists raised. Chase deliberately kept his hands open, arms at his sides. The first punch, if it came, rightfully belonged to Reidar. Physically, Chase had the advantage of height and weight on the other man. Even so, he knew better than to let his guard down. What Reidar lacked in brute force, he made up for in speed and dexterity. A black belt in martial arts, the ravenborn would lead with his deadliest attack.

Reidar worked his jaws. "I can't believe I have to say this to you of all people—"

"I can't quite believe it either." Chase replaced a mortified wince with cutting sarcasm. It was the dick move, but he was already batting o for 2, so why not?

"You'll shut up if you know what's good for you." Reidar talked louder, crushing Chase's retort. A visible vein throbbed at his temple.

"Shutting up." Chase took the warning at face value and pressed his lips together.

"Arabia is in jail because of you. How did this happen and what are your intentions?"

For a long moment, Chase stood there in stunned silence, his mouth hanging. Then he snapped straight to outrage and bellowed, "How the fuck is any of this my fault?"

"Simple, you got my little sister arrested—"

"Arabia got herself arrested."

"You should've prevented things from going this far."

"Prevented it? Arabia ambushed me with that spell..." Chase sputtered and bit his tongue. Talk about absolute bullshit! The roar of a wounded ego built in his chest. It'd annoyed him when Arabia had blamed him for her arrest, but hearing the same nonsense coming from Reidar only added insult to injury. By no stretch of the imagination did the convoluted conclusion make the least amount of sense.

"We both know Arabia is a creature of impulse, which is why you should've been watching out for her." Reidar projected an air of frayed patience; somehow implying that he bore the challenge of reasoning with an unreasonable person.

Patronizing and insulting.

Chase blew out a mighty huff and fumed.

Lunatics! The whole lot of 'em. Chase came within a hair's breadth of accusing Reidar, his sister, *and* the whole damn Jensen family of being a bunch of featherbrain madmen. For the sake of the respect he had for Reidar, he shut his mouth. It was a close thing, though.

Fortunately, life as a litigator had prepared him to compromise. Successful negotiations started with a concession, and then solicited one in return.

"Maybe there was something I could've done to mitigate the situation," Chase said, willing to give so he could get. "Explain to me how this is *all* my fault. Frankly, that part is eluding me."

Reidar screwed up his whole face. His mouth contorted as though he'd bitten into a sour lemon. Finally, he harrumphed. "Are you fucking with me, man?"

"No. Why would I fuck with you?"

"You've really no clue?"

"No clue." Chase quelled the impulse to spread his hands to demonstrate his utter cluelessness.

"Seriously?"

"Seriously."

"Huh." Reidar shook his head, clearly confounded by the extent of his friend's stupidity. The motion set his long hair to swaying. Even though

Chase understood the full extent of Reidar's genius when it came to manipulation, he still felt like an idiot.

Chase cleared his throat. "Reidar, what the hell is going on?"

"When ravenborn reach maturity, they go on Launching," Reidar began, adopting a dry, lecturing tone.

"I know what Launching is," Chase interrupted. "I don't need an education in your people's rites of passage."

"Apparently you do. Or at least you need a refresher. Launching ends for a ravenborn woman when she chooses a mate."

Chase was certain his chin hit the ground. His train of thought definitely flew straight off the tracks.

Reidar smirked, making it clear he derived pleasure from his friend's discombobulation. Without break, he continued, "It's customary for our women to initiate courtship, especially when she feels the man she wants has failed to notice her. To get his attention, she tricks him."

A great groan built in Chase's chest.

"Romantic trickery is usually small and relatively harmless. Unless, of course, the ravenborn woman feels neglected or believes the man to be particularly obtuse."

"What does it take to warrant a nuclear love spell?" Chase mumbled with marbles in his mouth.

"Dunno." Reidar smiled blithely and spread his hands. "I've never seen anything of this caliber before. None of my conspiracy has. You're all anyone is talking about right now. The commonly held opinion is that you're an incredible idiot to have provoked Arabia to this extent. They're calling you Moon Moon behind your back."

The silence stretched like warm taffy.

Moon Moon.

"Damn it." Chase smacked his hand to his forehead, and a moan tore from his throat. Talk about a head-on collision with a brick wall! Abruptly, everything made sense, starting with the love spell...

Well, almost everything.

"Light bulb just went on, huh?" Reidar asked dryly.

"Shit! How did I miss this?" He dragged his hand through his hair. Within, his wolf bounded with jubilant excitement. Oh boy! Arabia desired him as her mate! It required a conscious effort not to tilt his face to the sky and yodel in triumph.

"No clue." Reidar spread his hands in a you'redumber-than-can-be-believed expression of profound bafflement.

"I..." A rude thought interrupted Chase's boundless enthusiasm. Arabia wasn't a wolf. Their children might have feathers instead of fur. How would his pack react to their alpha taking a ravenborn mate? What would Chase's mother say?

"My dad had the same basic reaction." Reidar slanted a sly sideways glance, and his smirk said he'd read Chase's mind.

Heat suffused his face. Shame filled him for having indulged in such species nonsense even for a second. Wolf. Raven. It didn't matter. He'd love his children with Arabia regardless.... and his pack and parents would be delighted.

"What did Evelyn say?" Chase asked, clearing his throat. Not to disrespect Tobias, but the ravenborn queen's opinion carried more weight than her consort's.

"My mother is thrilled. Oh, and so is yours, too. They're already planning the wedding." Reidar grinned, and it wasn't nice. *Just. Plain. Mean.*

Chase delayed, pondering. Maintaining his guard, he asked, "How do *you* feel about Arabia marrying me?"

Reidar cocked his head. Unblinking, he stared

and then smiled. "It's fucking fantastic, brother," he said, grasping Chase's forearm. "I couldn't have chosen a better man for my sister. Congratulations."

"Thanks." Relief poured over Chase. He released a pent up breath. The friends slapped one another on the back and then separated.

"There's one more thing," Reidar began.

"Yeah, I know. Arabia is in prison." Chase fell into grim contemplation. An ominous shadow crossed Reidar's face. At a glance, Chase didn't need to cite the worst-case scenario. His blood brother understood.

If convicted, Arabia faced lifetime imprisonment... and Chase would endure loneliness until the day he died. Wolves paired for life. Now that he finally understood, no other woman could possibly become his soulmate.

"That's not what I meant. Besides, you'll take care of that." Reidar clasped his hands to Chase's shoulders and squeezed hard.

"I will?"

"Sure, you're going to put that legal eagle education of yours to good use and get Arabia released. Make sure you do something brilliant, or you'll never shake that Moon Moon tag."

Chase stifled a groan. "I appreciate the vote of

confidence. But clearing her name might be harder than you think."

"You don't have to clear her name. Just get her released." Reidar shrugged. Such cavalier indifference to the prospect of his sister going through life with a criminal record was so intrinsically ravenborn. Chase found his friend's *c'est la vie* attitude completely unfathomable. And distasteful. For the sake of diplomacy, he kept his thoughts to himself.

"C'mon, there's something I want to show you. It's about six miles from here." Reidar curled his fingers inward, a graceful sweep of flesh to feathers. His arm transformed to an ebony wing; a raven replaced the man. Thanks to his people's magic, his clothing shifted with him.

"Six miles? We could drive." Chase shoved his hands to his pocket, reaching for his car keys. He headed for his vehicle.

"Screw that!" Reidar rose on beating wings and released a mocking cackle. Fully shifted, ravenborn lacked vocal chords but they retained the ability to fully mimic human speech. Aside from their flight, it was the one thing Chase had always envied about them.

"Thanks but no thanks."

"Haven't you turned into a pampered pooch, Moon Moon? It used to be you were fit enough to run six miles!"

A snarl rolled Chase's throat, a distinct wolf's warning. He twisted his head to track the raven's progress. "Fly a little lower and call me that again!"

"Oohh, scary." Reidar landed on the roof of the silver sedan. His sharp talons sent him skidding across the icy metal before he found traction. When Chase opened the driver's side door, he squawked. "Seriously, are you really gonna drive?"

"I'll run. But first I need to stow my suit." Chase bit off with a grin. A roguish sense of adventure lifted his mood. He tugged at his tie, loosening the knot. As a rule, Stillwater's decorum called for its citizens to remain clothed while in public. Removing clothing to shift was allowed, however, so long as it didn't turn into public exhibitionism.

The raven produced a rude fart sound. "Pussy."

"Tweety."

"Moon Moon." Reidar flew off, effectively getting in the last word.

Chase grinned and shook his head. Fat chance he'd ever live *that* damn nickname down.

GRIFFIN DOOR

December 9th…

A heavy blanket of fresh snow covered the trees and the earth. Flurries of white descended from the grey clouds as the wolf and raven sped through the winter woods. In his avian form, Reidar glided overhead, usually in the lead but often circling back so he didn't leave Chase behind.

Hot breath poured from Chase's muzzle and coalesced into plumes of steam upon hitting the chilly air. He gathered himself, muscles bunching, and sprang into another lurch that carried him above the snowpack. His chest collided with the solid wall and he sank, only to repeat the whole process over again. Every leap advanced him another four feet forward, but he worked hard for every square inch.

His sides heaved and his muscles burned from the exertion, but it was a marvelous high. It'd been too long since he'd let his wolf out to play. Having his wolf in ascendance simplified everything. It felt so good and so right, he found himself wondering whether Arabia's accusations were right. Had he allowed his humanity, his urban lifestyle and career with all its trappings, to become a self-made prison?

In the late afternoon light, the pristine winter woods, the wolf and raven team presented the picturesque imagery perfect for a nature documentary. With Morgan Freeman narrating with that exceptional vibrato, *"In the wild, wolves and ravens have a complex symbiotic relationship that spans thousands of years. Watch now as this male raven swoops down to take a teasing pass at his four-footed companion."*

"Hey!" Reidar shrilled. He latched hold of the thick fur of Chase's ruff with his talons. Beating wings whapped against his ears. The unexpected assault knocked him straight out of his reverie, and Morgan Freeman's pleasant monologue came to an abrupt and grating end.

Chase growled and turned in a tight circle, trying to buck the bird on his back, but Reidar had a tight grip on his perch, which was well out of reach of snapping jaws. He completed at least three full rotations, however, chasing his own tail before he understood the futility of it. And it wasn't like he had any intention of actually eating Reidar...but the temptation did cross his mind. With a great grump, he halted and dropped his head, panting to catch his breath.

"Wff-wff," Chase coughed up in fair approximation of "What the fuck, dude?"

"Can you kick it up a notch? We don't have all day!" Reidar squawked.

Disbelief bubbled through Chase. He twisted out a Scooby-Doo approximation of, "We stopped so you could complain? You've got to be kidding me!"

Reidar produced a rude fart-whistle. "Have you figured out yet where we're going?"

"Durrr." Reidar glanced heavenward. Only about two miles ago! Obviously, they were on route to Arabia's bungalow. The knowledge filled him with trepidation. He hadn't been back there since the night they'd made love...and she'd been arrested. He'd self-deceived for a straight month, telling himself there wasn't any reason to go back. The truth was clear, cruel, and cringe-worthy. Chase had stayed away for one reason and one reason alone; he'd been too afraid to return.

Ghosts haunted him.

A cowardly alpha. Just the thought turned his stomach and caused him to question his self-worth. Did he deserve to be the leader of the Baron pack and the man the Princess of the Silverwind Conspiracy had chosen as her consort?

It crossed his mind to ask Reidar's opinion. Thankfully Chase's inability to speak prevented him from doing so before common sense kicked in. Reidar was his best friend and blood brother, but the ravenborn would've taken such a dumbass question as an invitation to ridicule without mercy. It would've been an act of monumental stupidity to offer more ammunition on a silver platter. So Chase kept his muzzle shut, and a good thing, too, because Moon Moon wasn't the name by which he wished to be known in perpetuity.

"Have you caught your breath yet?" Reidar asked.

Damn it. Thoroughly flummoxed, Chase heaved a deep sigh. He'd been tricked into taking a rest break. He should've suspected except he hadn't really wanted to examine Reidar's motivations too deeply. The run had felt good; yeah, he admitted it. He'd desperately needed the physical outlet...just like he'd benefitted from the imposed break.

"I'll take that as a yes. C'mon, it's at the top of the

hill." Reidar launched into the air, beating a deep rhythm with his wings.

Chase heaved to his feet and broke into a sprint, running a race against a raven. He stood no chance of winning, but he had to try anyway. When it came to him and Reidar the joy derived from their rivalry dynamic, not the win or lose. After so many years, he no longer kept score, and he doubted Reidar did either.

The uphill stretch proved the most difficult. At some point, the snow on the rocky slope had melted and refrozen. The slippery ice provided no traction. More than once, Chase's paws threatened to slide out from under him. He dug in his werewolf claws, drilling through the hoarfrost to gain purchase. It took him ten times longer to reach the crest than Reidar but that didn't matter. Satisfaction derived from the struggle, not the competition.

They reached the edge of the field that marked the backyard of Arabia's cabin. The trees were thinner there, so the back of the house was visible through the woods. Chase moaned and flopped onto his belly in the snow. A soft fall of flakes swirled from the sky, dancing in eddies, an incredibly pretty sight. Romantic. He desperately wished that Arabia were there to enjoy it with him instead of her brother.

"You okay?" Reidar sat on a low bough and turned a shiny black eye on Chase.

He woofed once. They had a communication system that dated to childhood: one bark for yes, two for no. Reidar's patronizing attitude rubbed him the wrong way, but he was smart enough to know that, too, was a matter of design. Tyr preserve him from meddling raven-shifters! But for the love of irony, they seemed to be inexorably intertwined with his destiny. At this point, fighting it seemed an exercise in futility.

"Good. Check this out." Reidar traipsed off the branch and glided to the ground. The raven alighted beside a patch of broken snow about two hundred feet from the house.

At a slow trot, Chase approached the trough. He halted a few feet from the nearest edge so he wouldn't disturb or damage whatever Reidar wanted to show him. Narrowing his eyes, Chase turned his attention to the indicated area.

Four deep, evenly spaced indentations broke the snow. Huge tracks. Whatever critter had left the impressions had avian talons in the front. It must've been one huge ass bird...or maybe a dinosaur. Had

Jurassic Park come to Stillwater? Or maybe some prehistoric survivor from the distant past? Not that Chase bought into the absurd speculation even for a second, but damn, that was one monstrous bird. Front prints aside, it was the rear tracks that created true consternation. The mysterious creature had enormous paws in the rear. Cat from the look of 'em. Maybe a lion or tiger...

A bird-cat beastie.

"What the actual fuck do you think this thing is?" Reidar asked, verbalizing Chase's exact thoughts down to the dot on the I and the cross on the T.

Chase coughed up another wolf-human hybrid sound, and then he pinned Reidar with an unwavering stare. He expected his look conveyed his explicit meaning better than any words. Skepticism danced through his mind. Was this a prank? Given the circumstances, it was in incredibly bad taste. All things being even, he found it difficult to believe Reidar would stage a twisted hoax while his sister was incarcerated.

The raven twitched his tail feathers. "No joke, or if it is, I'm being set up, too. Notice how the tracks just start here? Like the beast just dropped out of the sky...or something."

Or something was right.

On reflex, Chase scanned the surrounding area. A long furrow in the snow stretched out behind him, the trail he'd ploughed through the rime. In comparison, the bizarre bird-cat beastie appeared in the middle of the yard without any lead-up.

"I googled it," Reidar said, at the exact moment Chase arrived at the answer on his own. Without access to a computer or a library, he had no means of verifying it, but he could only think of one mythological monster said to be part eagle and part lion. From the tilt of Reidar's head, the ravenborn seemed to be following the same train of thought.

Chase barked. *Griffin.*

Simultaneously, Reidar declared, "It's gotta be a griffin."

The raven and wolf traded a long, loaded look. Searching regard—more questions than answers. A nonverbal dialogue passed between them.

Are you crazy?

No.

Well, am I?

I don't think so, but who's to say? Griffins went extinct centuries ago.

Yeah, well that's what they said about Bigfoot. We all know how that turned out.

What's next—the Loch Ness monster?

I refuse to answer that just on principle.

You have principles? Since when?

"Do you smell anything?" Reidar asked. "My sense of smell is all but nonexistent while I'm shifted."

Good question. He ought'a thought of that. Obligingly, Chase put his nose to the ground and inhaled deeply. A complex brew of scents flooded his nostrils: potent lion musk, the more subtle trace of an eagle, and it was decidedly male. He judged the tracks to be a few hours old, no more than twelve. Snuffling, Chase paced the edges of the trail. The brittle ice crunched beneath his paws and every step drew him closer to the house.

Foreboding gut-punched Chase upon arriving at the inevitable conclusion—the alleged griffin had set down and made a beeline straight for the back porch. His thoughts returned directly to all of the times Arabia had said that the love spell she'd cast could've only affected her and Chase. She'd *insisted* something else must be going on. But had he listened? No.

Should he have listened? Sure seemed like it.

Reidar hopped and flapped, skipping a few yards. "Well? Is it genuine?"

Chase barked once.

"Whoa, what has my sister gotten herself into this time?"

Chase snarled and gave a rough shake of his head. He had no clue what to make of any of it. The trace evidence—the spoor and the tracks—provided pretty solid proof of the existence of the bizarre amalgamation of bird and cat, though. But even that didn't confound or frustrate him even a quarter as much as Arabia's taciturn secrecy. If she alleged some third party's machinations, then surely she must have at least a sneaking suspicion of who was behind it. So why wouldn't she have told Chase everything?

"The back door is standing open. Let's check it out." Reidar took off without waiting for a reply.

Chase pursued, crossing the back yard in a few long strides and headed up the stairs onto the porch. As Reidar had observed, the entry to the house stood fully ajar. Chase crossed the threshold into a small laundry room.

Reidar perched atop the dryer and waited while Chase shifted to human. He completed the transformation crouched on the linoleum floor, fully naked, and more than a little uncomfortable. The second his fur receded, the cold assaulted his bare skin, and he shivered.

"Damn, it's cold in here," Chase complained the second he could speak.

"What'd you expect? No telling how long that door's been left open." Reidar cocked his head and hooted with avian laughter. "So tell me what you smelled."

"The scent is fresh. Not more than twelve hours." Chase shoved the door shut, and then opened the dryer, hoping to find something to wear. His search yielded a bath towel which he wrapped around his waist, knotted at his hip.

"And it's a griffin?"

"The spoor was an eagle-lion creature of some sort. Male."

"Thank you for being so specific and noncommittal, counselor. We wouldn't want you to have to speculate."

Chase snorted. "It was probably a griffin. Satisfied?"

"Never." Reidar whistle-laughed. "So, how do you suppose it fit in here anyway? That sure isn't a griffin door."

Chase opened his mouth, but his mind went blank. A cymbal clanged in his head and he groaned. "That was bad."

"No apologies. So?"

"He changed to human." Chase ran a bashful hand through his hair. Oh yeah. His wolf's acute sense of smell had detected that piece of info upon entering the house, but he'd filed it away without thinking about it. The sloppy oversight bugged him because he was anything but careless. Exactly the opposite, in fact. He was meticulous by nature.

"A griffin-shifter. Interesting. Have you met anyone in town who matches that description?"

"No, and I would've mentioned it if I had," Chase said with a sour grimace.

"Has Arabia ever told you about any griffins she knows?"

"I'd have mentioned that, too."

"Just checking." The raven hopped off the dryer and glided into the hallway.

"Yeah, yeah." He padded after Reidar, following him down the short corridor, which led to the tiny kitchen. Upon reaching the entryway, Chase stopped. The ravenborn clung to the stainless steel faucet, using it as a perch, but Chase barely noticed his friend.

The kitchen had been thoroughly ransacked. Cupboards and drawers emptied and the refrigerator left open. The remnants of broken plates and glasses covered the countertops and floors. From the rancid smell, the trash had been emptied and left to rot.

"Fuck," Reidar muttered darkly.

"Fuck is right. I'm going to kill whoever did this." Intense anger closed on Chase. His chest constricted, and his respiration shortened. Pain radiated from the spot right below his diaphragm. It burned. The violation of Arabia's home riled him up so much it might as well have been a trespass on Baron Pack territory.

Chase checked the rest of the house and found it to be the same shape as the kitchen. The intruder had torn apart everything in his path without any regard for Arabia's personal property or privacy. He'd even destroyed the mattress and bedding. This was one—of the many—places Chase and Arabia had made love.

His wolf bristled with aggression.

Fighting to contain his rage, Chase bent and picked up a pair of red panties on the bedroom floor. He closed his fist about the sexy garment while a storm brooded in his core. That griffin-bastard had touched these, too. It was the last straw. Right then and there, he swore himself to revenge.

"What do you think he was looking for?" Reidar asked from his roost atop the bedroom door.

"No idea but we'd better find out..." Chase trailed off, pondering what they knew and didn't. It occurred to him that maybe Arabia had provided all the relevant hints he needed. Once again, he just hadn't been listening.

"Ding ding ding! The lights just turned on. What'cha thinking?"

"That first night I got into town, the night of the spell, Arabia mentioned she'd dated some warlock—"

"Oh oh! The plot thickens!"

"Shut up." Chase frowned. "I assumed she was just trying to make me jealous. She claimed they'd been out on one date. She broke it off, but implied the warlock was an asshole about it."

"This looks like the work of an asshole."

Chase huffed in heartfelt agreement. "There's more to it than that..." He went on to describe the stranger who'd shown up at the Two Swans Inn and asked after him. "Grant said the man introduced himself as John, but Grant also thought the guy was lying."

"Huh. Do you think this John character is the same guy who did this?"

"Maybe..." Chase grimaced. Self-recrimination pinched him. He hadn't pursued the incident, and he should have investigated. That much was crystal clear. Oh, he had plenty of excuses. He'd devoted all his time and energy to Arabia's defense. But that didn't make up for the gross oversight.

"Stop beating yourself up," Reidar snapped. "Let's focus on what we can do to help my sister now."

"I can ask around town. Use my contacts to make some subtle inquiries. If there's a griffin in town, someone must know something," Chase said grimly. He might've been remiss in the past but no more. He intended to scrutinize every citizen of Stillwater, leaving no stone unturned. The investigation to come would make the Watergate investigations look like an ice cream social.

"Okay. I'll talk to my sister. Maybe she'll open up to me."

"Fine, you do that," Chase agreed, but grudgingly. The implication wasn't lost on him, and it chafed his pride.

Obviously, Reidar believed Arabia would trust her brother more than she did her lover. Thing was, Chase didn't really blame her. For weeks, he'd sensed she was holding something back, and it'd only made him angrier. Instead of working to earn her trust, he'd lashed out with recrimination and accusations. Hell, he even failed to recognize the love spell for what it was—the initiation of the ravenborn courtship ritual.

Chase blurted his thoughts aloud. "Fuck, I feel like an unbelievable idiot."

Reidar chuckled. "Cut yourself some slack. When it comes to women, it happens to the best of us."

"It's never happened to you." Chase shot his friend a nasty look.

"And it never will." Reidar puffed up his chest feathers.

"Someday, it will, and when it does, I'm gonna laugh my ass off."

"When pigs fly. C'mon, we've got our work cut out for us."

CHAPTER 11

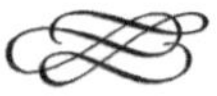

PRIVATE CAT'S EYES

December 10th...

At ten minutes before two a.m. Chase pushed open the front door of the Clover Club. An obese man in a lumberjack shirt stumbled past. He reeked of booze and BO. When Chase caught the underlying musk of elk, his wolf forced him to stop. Inexplicably, his predatory instincts aroused in a most impolite way. He pivoted, following the drunk's progress with piqued interest.

Swaying, the elk-shifter paused atop the three-step staircase. He grabbed his belly and released a mighty belch. The brisk winter wind whisked the stinky cloud straight over Chase's raised nose in an obnoxious olfactory assault. He grimaced and covered his face.

"Are you all right, Phil?" Laura's silken voice came from directly behind Chase. Simultaneously, the bartender caught his upper arm in a powerful grip, the very tips of her cougar claws sunk through his clothes and skin.

Caught unaware, Chase stiffened and swung around. His wolf ascended. He instinctively lowered his head and bared his teeth; his skin rippled over sinew in precursor to the shift. A warning rumble trembled in his throat.

Laura glared as only a cat could—unflinching and cool. Her eyes cast an eerie green glow across her firm features. No fear, only a dare.

Stalemate.

Chase had no intention of challenging Laura to a fight, so he backed down. Hell, he'd come here seeking her help. Even though it went against his nature as a dominant wolf, he averted his gaze and broke eye contact.

Laura twitched. Her basal aroma spiked with surprise, but she sheathed her claws and directed her attention over Chase's shoulder. "Did you hear me, Phil?"

"Yeah, I hear you! Damn it, Laura, you don't have to watch me," Phil complained. "I know I'm supposed to walk home when I'm this plastered. You already took my car keys. I don't need you tailing me, too. It's only three blocks, for gosh sake."

"And it's my job to make sure my customers make it home safe," Laura shot back. "So you'll just have to put up with me watching till you clear my property. This is an argument you're not going to win, so just skedaddle along." She jerked her head. "Go on. Git!"

Phil groaned and grumbled, but lurched down the stairs and got underway. Moving at a clip just above a tortoise's pace, he chugged off.

With a throaty huff, Laura held onto Chase. The insult stung—a stinging slap to his pride. What? Did she think he'd bound off after the lumbering elk-shifter, allowing his wolf free reign to hunt as instinct dictated? It sure seemed so. Laura waited until Phil disappeared around the corner of the building. Only then did she release Chase.

"A polite shifter society depends on predators not eating the prey." Laura placed a friendly pat on his chest.

"I wasn't going to eat him," Chase mumbled. Heat flushed his face. He would've bet money his ears were fire engine red. "Criminey, I was just looking."

"Chase-love, if I'd known that's what it takes to

turn your head, I'd have gained a hundred pounds and gotten sloshed ages ago." Laura laughed.

Chase blushed all that much harder and cursed his inexcusable primordial lapse. He had his reasons. It'd been an excruciatingly long day. Being bone-tired and frustrated, however, wasn't an acceptable excuse for salivating over a fellow sentient creature.

"The bar is closed, you know." Laura nudged him, drawing him back to the present. "Gotta say, I'm curious enough to sacrifice one of my nine lives— what the heck are you doing out at this hour?"

"I stay out late all the time." Chase tugged at his tie in a fit of discomfort. The stench of deceit clung to him. The cougar certainly smelled it, too.

"Sure you do. And I just *love* dogs and belly rubs." She snickered and pushed the door to the bar partway open. "You want to come inside?"

His mouth split in a reluctant grin. "Yes, please. I need to talk to you."

"All right then."

She ushered him inside and locked up behind them. Within, the lights were dimmed and the building empty except for the two of them. Somehow, Laura walked with a feline prowl despite being on two legs. She kept her head low and placed each step with deft precision.

Upon reaching the bar, she swept up a bowl of pretzels with a hooked hand as she moved along. All total, she gathered three or four containers of salty snacks, which she deposited behind the counter. Laura rolled her wrist in a flourish. "So, what's your trouble?"

"Do you still work as a private investigator?" Chase asked, settling his bulk atop a barstool across from her.

"I pick up the odd job here and there. Sometimes, I work as a PI, but more often than not, I'm just out picking up a bounty jumper." She patted the bar counter. "The Clover Club is what pays the bills."

"Ah, the unfulfilled aspirations of a wannabe Nancy Drew."

"That's Jane Tennison to you, buddy." She narrowed her eyes but then chuckled. "Why are you asking?"

"Would you consider taking me on as a client?"

Laura knit her brow. He halfway expected her to spout another of her corny come-ons, but she only cocked her head. "Doing what?"

"Local job."

"Those are my favorite." Her tone said otherwise. He wondered why she stayed in a town where she wasn't happy, but her personal affairs were none of his business. She set her phone on the bar. "Is it okay if I record this?"

"Sure." He paused to compose his weary thoughts. "A few days ago, a man came snooping around the inn where I've been staying," Chase said. "He asked a bunch of nosy questions and lied about knowing me."

"Backtrack a sec. Where are you staying?"

"The Two Swans Inn."

Recognition sparked in her gaze. "I know Grant and Maggie."

"Good, I'm sure they'll be happy to talk to you."

"Did this guy threaten the Wards?" She cracked her knuckles. When she flexed her fingers, the tips of claws protruded without shedding so much as a drop of blood. They slid right back beneath her skin again. Chase observed the display with veiled fascination. Such precise control was extremely rare in most shifter-species. He wondered whether the talent was common to all cats or a measure of Laura's self-discipline.

"No."

Disappointment flickered on her face. "All right, backtrack again and tell me more about the perp."

"He called himself John but Grant thinks he was lying." Chase went on to provide a physical description of the intruder. He got downright uneasy when he reached the next part. "According to my client, she went on a date with a warlock—"

"Hold up a sec. Your client?" Laura interrupted.

"Yes?" Chase tensed even more.

"Are you bound by attorney-client privilege from revealing her name?"

"It's Arabia Jensen." Chase braced for the worst. If the orgy-spell had caused Laura to do something she regretted... Well, that might come back now to bite him in the ass.

The cougar-shifter smiled with her lips sealed, an expression that did nothing to reassure him. His curiosity piqued, but whatever her secret, the cat held her tongue. Laura prompted, "So Arabia dated this warlock prior to her arrest?"

Jealousy cramped his gut. He disliked discussing Arabia's past romantic interests, but it had to be done. Uncharacteristically, Chase felt compelled to provide more information for context. But damn it, he didn't want Laura assuming his motivations were rooted in petty jealousy. "Yeah, they went on at least one date. Arabia refused to tell me his name. I do know he's a member of Pomegranate Fitness, and he was in her Pilates class. If you can obtain their membership roster, his information should be there."

"Mmm, a warlock who does Pilates. Maybe I should be paying you for this case." Laura licked her lips, the proverbial cat in the cream.

Chase pressed his lips together.

"Damn, who kicked your sense of humor to the curb, big guy?"

"Can you obtain the membership roster?"

"Sure, I can do that. Go on."

He talked. Laura interrupted to ask the occasional discreet question. She succeeded in drawing concrete details out of him, more information than he'd known he possessed. Her competence as an interviewer impressed him, enough so that he found himself thinking she'd have made a good attorney or police officer.

"Sometime yesterday, someone broke into Arabia's house and ransacked it," Chase said. "Clearly, they were searching for something, but I've no idea what or whether they found it. The intruder's tracks in the snow and his scent indicate he's a griffin. I believe—"

Laura's jaw dropped. "Hold it right there! You

can't just drop a bomb like that and just keep talking like we're discussing your horoscope."

Chase coughed to clear his throat. "I had a similar reaction, but the evidence was undeniable. You're welcome to check out the house for yourself."

"I'll do that. You can be sure," Laura assured him. She jerked her head and narrowed her eyes, the very vision of feline agitation. He got the distinct impression she knew more than she was saying, but he deemed it a bad time to press her.

"Like I was saying, I believe the warlock might be this griffin. There are circumstances associated with the case and how Arabia was apprehended that make me suspect his involvement may go even deeper than that."

"All right. What about magical scrying?"

He nodded. "Check for that, too."

"That'll run you extra."

"Do it."

"You think this this warlock-griffin is behind the orgy somehow, don't you?" Laura's gaze grew penetrating. She searched his face for clues.

Chase stayed silent and cast a pointed glance at the recorder. He refused to speculate while on tape. He'd been a lawyer long enough to be wary. Those sorts of things had a way of coming back to bite one in the ass. Instead, he reached into his pocket and dug out a key ring, which he set on the counter and slid to Laura. "I'd like you to sweep her house and my room at the B&B for bugs."

Laura considered him with a long look. In a thoughtful tone, she asked, "You're really going above and beyond. That raven has her talons in you, huh?"

"I'm just doing my job." Even Chase heard the lie in his voice. The further the criminal proceedings against Arabia progressed, the greater his sense of desperation. The last month of being separated from her had shown him a glimpse of what his future would be like without her—desolate and lonely. Wolves mated for life, and he, King of Fools, hadn't recognized Arabia for who she was to him until it was too late.

Laura snorted. She turned off the voice-recording application on her phone and tucked it away. "Okay, that should be enough to go on. If I think of anything else, I'll call."

"So you're taking the case?" Chase yawned against his fist.

"My rate is five hundred a day plus expenses. I require a thousand dollar deposit up front."

He balked. "That's highway robbery, even in Los Angeles."

She gave him the side eye. "This ain't Los Angeles, and I ain't no chump. Warlock-griffins have got to be dangerous."

Chase couldn't argue, so he handed her the last word...and his credit card.

THOU SHALL NOT KILL THY BROTHER

December 10th...

Arabia loved her brother, but that didn't stop her from wanting to kill him.

"Do you have anything to say?" Reidar queried in that impatient tone he affected with people he thought were damn fools.

Arabia squeezed her eyes shut and buried her face in her hands to keep from reaching for his throat. She wasn't angry. More like fed up with the men in her life. *All* men. Chase and Reidar were two peas in a pod with their determined allegations and irrational conviction that she was some sort of superlative trickster. No matter how many times she denied it, they refused to believe her.

"A griffin broke into your house and ransacked it.

We have no idea what he was looking for or whether he found it. Whatever's going on, Chase needs to know if there's any chance it'll help your defense," Reidar said, pretty much repeating what he'd already said for the fourth time. Maybe he hadn't heard her three adamant denials. Or perhaps he hoped her answer would undergo a miraculous metamorphosis.

Arabia ran her fingers through her hair and exhaled mightily... *Must. Not. Commit. Fratricide.* At least, not while they were in the prison visitation center where it would be witnessed by guards and caught on camera. Early Monday morning meant the area was empty except for her and Reidar. Chase would be at court doing some sort of pre-trail mumbo jumbo. In his defense, he'd explained each step of the judiciary timeline and process to her in great detail. She'd listened and nodded, but it'd all turned to gobble-gook in her head. All that really mattered to her was the reality of her continued incarceration...and the possibility it could become permanent.

"Arabia, are you listening to me?"

"Yes, Reidar. I'm listening, and you're repeating yourself. I don't know what you want me to say." She flipped her bangs back and grasped the heavy gold hair bead at the base of the braid below her ear. She worried it between her fingers.

"You don't seem concerned."

"Concerned? I'm not." Arabia tipped back so the hard plastic chair balanced on its rear legs. The precarious, wobbly position matched her mood perfectly.

"Why not?" Reidar cocked his head, tucking his chin, the classic ravenborn look of askance. She knew it well. That expression usually preceded accusations—she'd stolen his stuff, messed with his stuff, or bubble wrapped the family's pet dog. Thing being, she was usually guilty. For once, she actually was one-hundred percent innocent.

Good luck convincing Reidar of that.

"Why not what?" Arabia chose to redirect.

He twitched. "Why," he said with exaggerated patience, "aren't you worried?"

"Because, dear brother, I'm stuck in here." She released the gold bead and tapped the tabletop with her ragged nail. "I have no control over what happens out there, so there's no point in getting worked up. And I'm sure if a griffin breaks into prison with the intention of harming me, the guards are obligated to protect me."

She frowned and cast a wary glance at the

sentries stationed at the entrances to the visitation center. Frankly, she doubted any of the guards made enough money or had a strong enough sense of duty that they'd place themselves in harm's way for an inmate. She hoped it never came down to that, because she didn't want to put it to the test.

"Besides, I'm not sure I even believe in griffins," Arabia added when Reidar failed to respond. "If it would make you feel better, I could lie and make something up."

"You need to stop being so damn flippant."

"Too late for that!"

"Damn it, Arabia! This isn't a game. Your freedom is at stake—"

"You think I don't know that? This is my life, not yours!" She smashed the chair down onto all fours. "I'm sorry, but I don't know anything at all about a griffin or why he'd want to take apart my house. I wish I did! It'd be fantastic if there actually was some huge secret that would help get me out of here, but there's not."

"Nothing?" Reidar searched her face with quiet desperation. He loved her. She knew that. No matter how annoying, his persistence sprang from genuine affection, and so she had to forgive him for being a jerk.

"No, nothing. I'm sorry." She shook her head, and he pressed his lips together.

A drawn out delay ensued.

"What about the guy you dated?" Reidar asked out of the blue.

"Chase and I never really dated—"

"No, the warlock from your gym."

Arabia lifted her chin and considered it. "Why on Earth do you think Damian Charming might be behind the burglary?"

"Damian Charming," Reidar repeated. "That's his name?"

She shrugged. "Yeah, but it doesn't matter."

"He was stalking you. Maybe he's behind all this."

"Oh, that!" Arabia blew out her cheeks and ducked her head.

"Oh, that?" Reidar repeated in a tone of cutting sarcasm. He stared straight through her—the gaze of an older brother who understood a kid-sister's tricks only too well.

Heat swept her face. She forced herself to hold his gaze. "Damian and I went out on one lousy date." She held up her finger. "One. That was it. We had no chemistry together. The guy is so uptight he makes

Chase look laid back. I honestly can't think of a single reason he'd have to stalk me."

Reidar stabbed the air hard enough to hammer a nail. "That's not what you said in your message."

"I may've taken certain liberties but it was only because I needed to be sure Chase would take notice. In a twisted sort of way, I actually have Damian to thank for making me realize..." She trailed off, unable to say the rest aloud.

"What's that?" Reidar mumbled. An internal battle waged on his face, she supposed between ire and anger. Right about then, he probably wanted to throttle her, and she didn't blame him in the least.

"Damian made me realize how much I need Chase. After that disastrous date, I concocted the whole scheme for luring him to Stillwater." She felt a little bit guilty about that, but not very. It'd been a good plan, and it'd worked like a charm.

"But Damian Charming never harassed you?"

"Not that I'm aware of." Arabia tilted toward caution, choosing language to hedge her bets. Really, she couldn't say what the warlock did or didn't do in his free time. For all she knew, Damian had a creepy stalker shrine dedicated to her. But she doubted it.

Reidar slumped into disappointment. "That sucks. He was our best lead."

"I'm sorry." She hung her head in genuine guilt...and real fear. She desperately wished she had something useful to tell her brother. She was counting on him and Chase to save her.

He heaved a deep sigh. "I'd better go tell Chase what I didn't find out."

"I'm scared, Reidar." Arabia crossed her arms over her chest, holding herself tight. She longed to hug her brother but touching between inmates and guests was forbidden.

Reidar set his face to a stony mask. "Chase will figure this out."

But what if he doesn't? Arabia couldn't bring herself to ask. She preferred not to know the answer anyway.

CHAPTER 13

COMMITTED TO CRAZY

December 17th…

Waiting had never been Arabia's strength. Doing it in a small, enclosed space triggered her claustrophobia in the worst way possible. She dragged one of the pair of school-style chairs away from the table, placed it in the corner, and sat. The room bore the unmistakable mark of a soulless government building with its taupe walls and threadbare carpeting that smelled moldy. Barren walls, except for the ticking round clock, which claimed it was 6:48 p.m. She measured her sanity in its clickety-clack as the seconds ticked past.

Two corrections officers had plucked Arabia from the exercise yard where inmates were permitted an hour of exercise after dinner. Without explanation, the guards shoved her into a white transport van. Her many questions went unanswered. She'd gotten a brief glimpse at the prodigious facade of the Stillwater City Courthouse before they'd escorted her inside. On the second story, they shoved her into her current cage and closed the door. The key-turned lock rotated with an ominous thunk, securing her in a prison that didn't even have a thin window to gaze out.

An eternity passed and the merciless clock counted off fifteen minutes. With each tick-tock, the walls closed another millimeter. Arabia turned some figures over, trying to estimate fidgeted distance and volume, but she had no head for numbers. She had no idea how long she had left or whether she'd run out of air before this trash compactor pulverized her to a pulp. She preferred suffocation to being crushed if that's what it came down to, but she worried Chase would never learn how she'd died. A month from now, would some hapless janitor find her powdered bones?

Sixteen minutes... Scuffing emerged from the other side of the entrance. Arabia tensed as a key inserted and the lock turned. The door swung open, revealing Chase's familiar form. As he entered, he said, "I'm sorry I'm late. It took me ten minutes to figure out where they'd put you..."

"Chase!" Arabia launched from her perch and flew into his arms. With a muffled sob, she wrapped her arms around his chest and buried her face against his throat. Hot tears of relief and joy wet her cheeks.

"Hey!" Chase dropped his briefcase and tightened his arms around her. "What's wrong?"

"Oh, Goddess, I thought I was going to die alone in here." She trembled like a flamingo in a blizzard and snuggled closer to Chase. His heat provided her only source of warmth. And he smelled so good. She felt safe again for the first time since she'd been arrested.

"Shh, you're safe. I've got you." He stroked his strong hands over her hair and shushed her. He stared past her into the miniscule conference room and then swore softly beneath his breath. "Damn it! I provided explicit instructions that you were to be taken to the small courtroom."

"Yeah, well, apparently those goons who brought me here aren't so good at following directions," Arabia snapped, struggling to recover her aplomb. Under his soothing touch, her shaking gradually ceased.

"Come on." Chase set Arabia on her feet but kept

a protective arm wrapped around her shoulders. He swooped to retrieve his briefcase, and then dragged her into an empty hallway.

"Where are we going? Won't you get in trouble for just taking me?"

"Taking you where you were supposed to go in the first place? No, I don't think those two bozos who misplaced you will complain. Not if they want to keep their jobs," Chase scoffed. His long strides ate up ground at a furious pace. She had to jog to keep up. They traveled along long corridors, mostly deserted, and passed only a few people.

"You're so sexy when you go all badass lawyer!" Arabia only snickered because she needed her wind just to keep up with him. Not that she minded. It felt good to stretch her legs without worrying that a trigger-happy guard would assume she was making an escape attempt and shoot her.

They descended a flight of stairs and approached a pair of double doors. The plaque read: Small Courtroom. Chase shoved one door open and held it for her. Arabia entered, and he followed her into an area the equivalent of a decent-sized auditorium, unoccupied other than for them. It had the usual setup: a judge's bench, witness stand, and a court reporter's cubby. Jury box to one side, tables for the prosecution and defense. Oh, and a towering white marble statue of a blindfolded woman holding a set of scales in one hand and a long sword in the other.

Arabia understood the symbolism—justice is blind. But frankly, she got damn edgy at the prospect of some sightless lady hacking her way through life with a weapon that size. Anyone unfortunate enough to get in her way might get chopped down.

"What're we doing here?" Arabia descended the gentle slope of the aisle, turning to survey the neat rows of seats. With a touch of envy, she regarded the high ceilings.

"I've got it reserved for three hours for an attorney-client conference. It's all ours until the courthouse closes at ten." Chase set his case atop the defendant's table. "You can shift and stretch your wings—"

"Really?" Arabia lit up with hope and fear. It sounded too good to be true but Chase wouldn't lie to her. Not about this.

"Really." He nodded and smiled, looking inordinately proud of himself. For once she didn't mind his insufferable ego. He deserved to be smug.

"Thank you! Thank you so much!" She flew to him on fleet feet and cinched her arms about his waist in a joyous hug. This time, Chase raised his arms in a startled reflex before he returned her embrace. He did so cautiously, as though her affection might be a trap, and she didn't really blame him. Last they'd parted, it'd been in anger following yet another of their countless arguments. Chase wasn't like her—he held onto grudges with clenched jaws.

Touching him lit a fever on her skin, an insatiable thirst she couldn't quench in their current circumstances. The banked fire in her core sparked. Out of self-preservation, she stepped back. She held up her arms, displaying the slim shift-deterrent bracelets that hung on her wrists. "What about these?"

"Let's get those off you." He dug a magical key out of his pocket, a three-inch steel wand of disruption, which she'd seen only in the possession of guards and police officers before.

She hesitated. "Where did you get that?"

"Let's say I have friends in high places." He cracked a smile but when she didn't laugh, he sighed. "It's legit. Judge Ramses awarded me temporary custody of you."

"So you're my keeper?"

His smile turned wry. "I've always been your

keeper. Since you were three and tried to jump off the roof of the house before you'd learned to shift."

"You caught me," she said softly.

Even as a little girl, she'd believed in Chase Baron. A few precious, exhilarating seconds of free fall. She'd taken that leap without hesitation, knowing Chase would catch her before she hit the pavement. And he had. Ever since then, her leaps of faith had grown more daring. Risked more. This last one with the love spell had been a doozy. Her freedom, more important than her life, hung in the balance. It made her wonder whether he'd be able to save her this time. For the first time, she questioned her actions. In silence, their gazes locked, and they stared into one another's souls. Tension lines radiated from the corners of Chase's eyes and mouth. She perceived his worry and doubt. Fear coursed through her.

"What happens if you remove my cuffs and I just take off?" Arabia asked, mostly to gauge his reaction to the question. *Mostly...* Of course the thought crossed her mind.

"Fleeing from imprisonment is a crime. You'd be a fugitive for the rest of your life." Chase provided a cool, measured answer. He was speaking not as her friend or lover but as an attorney... *her* lawyer.

Realization rocked her—he'd anticipated this.

"Maybe that wouldn't be so bad." She tilted her head, studying him.

"Maybe it wouldn't." His expression remained dead serious. "You'd have to live off the grid and stay on the move."

"Not all that different from my life before prison." Ravenborn tended to lead bohemian lifestyles. For every member of her breed who remained in one place, another subscribed to a philosophy of wanderlust.

"This is all hypothetical, of course. I'm speaking as your attorney and advising against pursuing an unwise course of action."

"Of course," she said, tongue-in-cheek, and at last he smiled.

It faded fast.

"Would you be held responsible if I fled?" Arabia asked softly and quite unnecessarily. Of course he'd get in trouble. The real question—how much? Chase's status as the Alpha of the Baron Pack should afford him some protection, but Stillwater was hundreds of miles and a world removed from Los Angeles.

"Don't worry about me. This is about you."

"Don't be stupid. Of course I have to worry about

you." Angry tears pricked her eyes. She looked away to conceal them. Did he really believe her so selfish that his welfare meant nothing to her?

"Fleeing means you'd always be a wanted criminal," Chase warned, sliding into that brisk, all-business mode again. "It means forfeiting whatever shot you have now at an early verdict or a mistrial. Even if I managed to clear the charges against you—"

"What are the odds I'll be found innocent?" Arabia asked. Chase sealed his lips. When he hesitated to speculate, she prompted him. "Come on. I know you've got an informed opinion. Give it to me straight up."

His gaze hooded. "The odds you'll be found innocent are slim to none."

She swallowed around the stinging hardness, like a hailstone struck her in the throat, and struggled to speak clearly. "And the odds of a mistrial?"

"That depends on a lot, especially the testimony of the arresting officer. A lot will turn on his credibility on the stand, and that's difficult to predict. There is a gaping hole in the means by which you were found out and apprehended: that anonymous caller who notified the police that you'd cast the spell."

This again. Arabia clenched her fists, anticipating what he'd say next.

"Do you have any idea who that might've been?"

"No, no clue." Her answer emerged curt and clipped, but damn it! He'd only asked her the same darn question about a hundred thousand times, and her response remained unchanged.

"Arabia, I need you to think. This is important. It would really help if you could give me something... anything." His tone was charged with impatience and his jaw hardened, mere hints of his mindset. The man had a glacial countenance. For the ten percent of his true emotions revealed, the other ninety percent remained concealed.

"There's nothing—no one. I didn't tell anyone what I was up to."

"I need you to think. Could someone have deduced what you were up to from the components you purchased?"

"I bought flowers, Chase. *Flowers.* I told Mrs. Bee they were for the scented sachets I sell in my shop, and most of the time that's all I used them for."

"What about Ceridwen's Tears?"

"They were a gift from the goddess direct. So unless you think Ceridwen wanted to set me up—in which case, I'm royally fucked—then, no. No one I can think of had the means or the motivation to anticipate what I was up to. I'm sorry. I really am. I'd love to be able to give you something if it would get you off my case."

Arabia shut her mouth but not fast enough.

"Is that what you really want? To get me off your case?" Fury smoldered on Chase's handsome face, and real fear lanced through her. Even if she mortgaged her soul, she couldn't afford a lawyer of his caliber. If he dropped her, the court would assign a paid public defender of questionable competence to her case.

She'd be screwed.

The walls of reality were closing around her again. While the courtroom wasn't an enclosed space, it represented the people and the system that sought to deny her freedom. Claustrophobia threatened to send her into a panic. No hope of escape from her inevitable fate—to be sucked under, ground to a pulp, and spat out again.

She hiccupped on a suppressed sob and put her hands together. "I didn't mean that! I'm sorry. Please don't give up on me even if I deserve it. I know I'm a brat. I know I'm crazy, but I need you."

Chase softened. He handed her a handkerchief. "I'm not going to abandon you, Arabia. Not ever." A slow smile spread on his face, and he made a too obvious but sweet attempt to cheer her up. "I'm one-hundred percent committed to your kind of crazy."

"Thank you." Arabia laughed and sobbed, scrubbing away tears with the hanky. Damn her eyes, they just wouldn't stop leaking. Chase Baron was the sweetest, most loyal man alive, and she prayed she would prove worthy of his dedication. "I hope my crazy doesn't get us both committed."

CHAPTER 14

FREEDOM FLIGHT

Chase ran his hand through his short hair, disrupting his neat appearance. "It's almost eight. I'm sorry for wasting an hour of your time rehashing this again."

"An hour of my time with you is never a waste. I know you're only trying to help me." She hung her head in shame, feeling like a terrible ingrate.

"Hold out your arms," Chase instructed, and she obeyed, pressing her wrists together. He passed the iron wand over the enchanted bracelets that prevented her from shifting. The latches popped open.

Without a word, Arabia removed the cuffs and passed them to Chase. She rubbed her wrists as though to restore feeling, even though the bracelets had been loose. She still hadn't decided whether to flee.

"One more thing," Chase said as she began to undress. While she actually possessed the magic necessary to shift and take her clothing with her, she refused to make the coarse prisoner uniform a part of herself.

"Yes?" Arabia asked, her voice muffled as she dragged her shirt over her head. Her pulse raced and she fumbled in her urgency to shed the restrictive garments.

"There are a lot of strange, unexplained things going on."

"Such as?"

"Such as on December 5th, a man came by the bed and breakfast where I've been staying. He was asking nosy questions. He gave a false name and lied to the landlord about knowing me. Days later, a griffin-shifter ransacked your house. We still don't know what he was looking for or if he found it."

Arabia clutched her shirt over her bare breasts. She pondered, absently tilting her head to the side in a very ravenesque manner. Speculation raced through her mind. It'd been a week since Reidar had interrogated her on these same matters. Chase had never brought it up before, so it seemed doubly weird that he'd chosen to broach the topic *now*. Without a doubt, her brother had repeated everything she'd said to Chase. And he must suspect she'd assume they'd talked and so on and so forth. Up, up, and away into that infinity and beyond of misgiving and conjecture that went with 'knowing'.

Such things never ended well.

The silence dragged on. Eventually, Chase cleared his throat. "Arabia," he said in his lawyer-voice, "you didn't answer my question."

"Technically, you didn't ask one, counselor. Whatever it is I'm accused of this time, I deny everything. And I have a great alibi. I've been locked up for the last month."

He bared his teeth without smiling. "I wasn't accusing you of anything."

Arabia blew her bangs out of her face. "No? 'Cause that's the tone you always use when you're about to."

Chase gave the appearance of a man struggling to retain his patience. He started again, "It's not my intention to make accusations. I'm simply trying to understand."

"Stop. Right there." Arabia thrust her hand out and unwittingly tossed her top onto the floor. It landed at Chase's feet. His gaze dropped to her bare breasts and got stuck there. In her indignity, she barely noticed. "I'm going to tell you the same thing I told Reidar. Damian and I went out *once*. I can't think of a single reason he'd have for visiting your B&B under an alias. To the best of my knowledge, he has no known connections to any griffins. I don't know any griffins either, so I've no clue why one trashed my place."

"Did you know Damian Charming is a cop?"

She blinked and her lips parted in surprise. It took a moment to recover her poise. "Yes, of course. He told me before we went out on a date."

"And you didn't think something like that was worth mentioning?"

"Frankly, no." Arabia removed her socks and shoes. Her clothing lacked the allure of a belly dancing costume, but one would never have guessed based on the way Chase followed her every movement with rapt fascination.

It was damn satisfying.

A seductive shimmy of her hips sent her pants and underwear slithering down her hips. Garments puddled about her ankles, leaving her gloriously naked and freed of all constraints.

Chase's gaze roamed the curves of her body with the weight of a lover's caress. In a low, throaty voice, he said, "This is exactly why I'm asking questions. You didn't think it was relevant to mention you'd dated a police officer, so I'm wondering what else got left out. I know I'm going to regret saying this, but I have to ask what the hell was going through that beautiful bird brain of yours."

A smile curved her lips. "Okay, fine, but you can't say I didn't warn you. You know Damian and I met in a Pilates class. Honestly, I was way more interested in that ripped, gorgeous body of his than what he did for a living."

Chase narrowed his eyes and lowered his head—a predator's stalking stance. *Ooohhh, dangerous...* Delicious shivers coursed through her. He growled, "You're baiting me."

"Of course I am. I love it when you get all grr-growly." Arabia sashayed closer, swaying her hips. She placed her hands flat against his chest. His heart throbbed strong and proud. A ferocious wolf in lawyer's clothing.

"This is serious," Chase grumbled. Primal aggression burned in his eyes and his basal scent grew muskier. "Suppose Damian Charming is behind it. Can you think of anything at all that might relate to what he'd be after?"

"Nope." She rolled her shoulders so her cleavage

lifted and her taut peaks abraded on the fine wool of his suit coat. "I haven't seen or spoken to Damian in over a month. Maybe he's following the trial and decided to check you out. Maybe he needed legal advice..."

"Maybe he's jealous."

"Maybe you're jealous." Arabia fisted his tie and tugged. With a miniscule effort, she pulled him down to her. His pupils dilated, eclipsing the colored parts of his eyes, and his hot breath blew over her skin. She marked the exact moment she lost control to him.

Chase grasped her shoulders tightly and smashed his mouth over hers. He thrust his tongue deep, claiming her with primitive possessiveness. His touch lifted her to heights that she'd only ever reached before via flight. If nothing else, her ruinous love spell had this one silver lining—it provided the key that unlocked his passion. Trouble sprung from confinement. And like Pandora of legend, Arabia had a stubborn determination to make sure the beast never got put back in the box.

Their embrace broke, leaving her panting. In a velvety voice, she said, "You don't have any reason to be jealous. If I'd wanted Damian, I only had to crook my finger and he'd be mine. You, on the other hand..." She swallowed around the lump in her throat. "I had to resort to magic to even catch your attention."

"No, you didn't." Scary intensity darkened his gaze. That look made her feel like the only woman in the world—the only woman in *his* world. Her heart beat in triple time, outpacing itself until she imagined tiny feet falling all over themselves.

Oh, hearts should have wings. Poor distressed things...

"Oh, didn't I?" She meant it as a quip, but even she couldn't miss the note of pleading in her voice. She craved reassurance almost as much as she wanted him.

"No." He stroked her hair, pushing it out of her face.

"No?"

"No." His breath blew across her cheek in a soft caress,

She missed the exact moment he bent and covered her mouth. Their lips clung and tongues danced. His zesty flavor set her taste buds on fire, like consuming a super-hot pepper sauce. It hurt so good —mixed pleasure and pain—and she had to have more. Abruptly, she tipped straight into a boiling cauldron of arousal and need.

Arabia reached for his fly. He'd worn that belt again, the one with the overly complicated buckle that seemed to have been designed specifically to thwart her. She seized hold of it and tugged, but the damn thing defied her attempts to loosen it. For the first time in her life, she regretted not having claws or she'd have slashed straight through the leather. Finally, with a frustrated cry, she broke the kiss and swooped down, bringing his crotch to eye level. A promising bulge filled out the front of his trousers, her prize if she could only get past the barrier.

"You seem to have a problem here, Big B."

He groaned and chuckled. "That's one way of putting it."

"I'll give you a hand with that... if I can ever get your damn belt off. What the hell is this thing—a chastity belt?" She complained, fumbling with it.

"Arabia, are you sure?"

"Absolutely." A glad sound escaped her lips when she finally defeated the infuriating contraption. She made quick work of the top button and zipper that barred her way.

"This will cut into your flight time." Despite his admonition, he cooperated fully with her efforts to undress him. Chase shoved his pants and trunks down off his hips, freeing his erection.

"It's not even a question." Given a choice between being with Chase and anything else, she'd always choose him.

His long, thick cock jutted forth from a nest of curls. His scrotum hung heavy, swollen with blood. When he shuffled a step, his dick swung slightly in a graceful motion that reminded her of how a male raven would've bobbed his head during courtship. A giggle escaped her.

"What's so funny?"

"Nuthin'." Arabia wrapped her hand around the base of his shaft and slid her other beneath to cradle his hefty balls. She loved how he filled up and even overflowed her palm, and she reveled in the lusty groan that tore from his throat.

"That ain't nuthin', woman." He moaned, a low and lusty sound, and rolled his hips. The thrust bumped the hood of his cock against her chin.

She snickered. "Oh my, yes, that is something!"

"Stop." Chase fisted locks of her shoulder-length hair and pulled her to him. He pressed his member against the seam of her mouth. His musky scent flooded her nostrils. Salty precum slickened her lips.

"Are *you* sure about this? We are in a court of law, counselor. I'd hate to have to feel guilty about leading you astray again." Arabia taunted him with his own words. She placed a kiss on the crown of his cock, smoothing the glossy flats of her teeth over him.

"I'm sure." Chase chuckled, telling her she'd made her point. But that didn't stop her from wanting to really rub it in and make him suffer.

"Maybe we should discuss the finer points of what we're agreeing to. That way no one feels tricked." She flicked the notch on the underside of his penis with the tip of her tongue, stroking that exquisitely sensitive spot.

"Arabia..." He said her name as a warning. A snarl rolled from his throat, and she damn near twittered with glee.

"Yes, Chase?" She put on her best angel face and gazed up at him with wide-eyed innocence. She had the upper hand—quite the feat considering she was on her knees.

"Shush up. I'm going to fuck your mouth. Open." He growled the command. The husky reverberation sent a visceral thrill through her.

Arabia parted wide, eager to take all of him. She secured a firm grip on the back of his buttocks, digging her fingernails into the iron-hard sinew beneath his soft skin. She wrapped her lips about the mushroom-shaped head. He tightened his hold on her hair and eased in slowly.

Arabia produced a muted protest in the back of her throat. Arousal smoldered in her core. Her nipples were hard and erect, so sensitive that even the drafty air currents of the courthouse agitated them. She clenched her thighs together, seeking even the slightest relief for the ache between her legs—an emptiness begging to be filled.

"Easy, I want to savor this. I've been fantasizing about this for years," Chase murmured.

He had? She arched her brow, bursting with curiosity. Only a muffled grunt escaped. So hard to talk with her mouth full. Besides, her mother had always said it was bad manners. She swirled him like an ice cream cone and lapped the ridge along the underside of his shaft. He rocked his hips, pushing the dome of his shaft into the pouch of her cheek. He tasted clean and bright in addition to his piquant heat.

His abdominal muscles clenched and unclenched in a rhythm that matched the contraction of his scrotum. No matter what he claimed about making it last, the man wasn't long for this world.

Greedily, she sucked harder, drawing in her cheeks, and gripped his buttocks tighter. Tilting her head back, she altered the angle of his entry. His next thrust brought him deep into her throat. A loud, startled bellow tore from Chase and his member twitched within her mouth. She was positive he'd climax, so it came as a shock when he pulled out without coming.

The world spun. Arabia found herself swept off her feet, hauled across the room, and dropped onto her hands and knees. With a gasp, she tossed her hair out of her eyes and looked around to assess her surroundings. She found herself staring straight at a pair of white marble bare feet.

Chase's muscular bulk covered her from behind. His huge hands locked about her waist, and the length of his erection probed the cleft of her buttocks. Arabia squeaked, clutched the statue's base, and held on for dear life. Oh, for the love of feathers, it was a good thing Lady Justice had her blindfold on! The things Chase Baron was doing here would've scandalized that proper dame.

He stroked his thick length across the lips of her drenched pussy and nudged her clit. Without warning, she clenched. A towering wave of pleasure crashed over her. A wail ripped from her, and she succumbed to a sudden and violent orgasm. Her juices soaked his swollen shaft and the insides of her thighs. Before she came down off the high, another tsunami engulfed her. Her voice soared in flight.

"Scream for me, Princess. That's what I want to hear." Chase produced the guttural grunt in conjunction with a growl. Against her, his entire body throbbed with pent-up aggression. From the feel of how rigidly he held himself, every muscle of his powerful body must have been drawn taut.

"Chase, please." Arabia arched her back and tilted her pelvis in a desperate bid to have him inside of her. Stars danced before her vision. Her heart fluttered like a bird determined to escape its cage, and the rasp of their harsh breathing resembled a raven's song.

"You're mine. Say it." His rough hands spanned her waist. He positioned the broad head of his cock against her entrance and pushed forward, claiming one excruciating inch at a time. He parted and penetrated her pussy, stretching her to the limit.

"I'm yours," Arabia all but sobbed. "I've always been yours." She shuddered and strained to overcome his restraint, attempting to force him to take her hard and fast. His strength, however, both mental and physical, far exceeded hers. He maintained mastery, claiming her on his own terms.

"Gods, you're so damn tight, Arabia. You feel

fucking fantastic." Abruptly, he poured on a burst of speed and slammed into her with a powerful thrust. Their hot, sweaty flesh slapped together with a pronounced smack. The impact bounced her breasts, and she'd have landed on her face if not for his support.

An ecstatic cry warbled in her throat. Whatever smart-ass remark she'd been about to make vanished from her lips and thoughts. Wanton with need, she rocked against him. Every thrust carried her higher. Immense tension gathered within her, building toward an inevitable and fantastic explosion. They came together like a storm, creating furious lightning and booming thunder. Thor couldn't have done it any better.

With a lusty grunt, Chase nudged aside her damp hair and pressed his lips to the side of her throat. His hot breath puffed across her sweaty skin. His teeth grazed her throat in a light mating bite, but he didn't draw blood. Her heart damn near flew out of her chest because she couldn't reach him to return it. Then, the flair of his cockhead hit her sweet spot and the whole world flew apart. Arabia wailed at the top of her lungs. Her body shook in the throes of climax.

Rapture.

Behind her, Chase roared in triumph and followed her over the precipice. His entire frame grew rigid with the strain of exertion. His hands clenched on her waist hard enough to hurt, but pain was light-years beyond her. He pumped into her a few more times and then found his own release, spilling his hot seed into her.

Afterward, he collapsed on top of her, crushing her beneath his weight. She didn't mind. She loved the closeness and cherished every moment of intimacy. Fully sated, she remained contentedly beneath him.

"If you want to fly, you'd better shift before I recover." Chase rolled onto his side, propping his head on his bent arm.

"That's a tough choice." She flipped over onto her back and gazed up at him. He looked relaxed with a rare, wide smile on his face. Happy. It thrilled her to know that she'd been the one to bring him such joy.

Arabia cupped his chin and kissed him long and soft. "I can't run if it means running away from you too. Not when all I want to do is run to you."

Chase opened his mouth, but she feared his reply too much to wait for it. Arabia raised her arms and shifted to a raven. The sharp tips of quills punctured her fingertips as her arms altered to wings. Black plumage sprang out across her skin and she rapidly shrank. She sprang and rose on beating wings.

Summoning her raven magic, she conjured a stiff breeze. It gusted through the courthouse, carrying the scent of elemental air magic—crisp and clean like spring rain. She flew as high as the ceiling allowed and then swooped low over the auditorium seating. The confines of the courtroom prevented her from going high or far, but even limited flight was glorious.

Her conflicted, complicated lover watched her from below, tracking her progress. She wouldn't try to escape. Fleeing from justice meant running from Chase. The man had a settled life with a pack and a career. He'd never give up everything to go on the road with her, and she'd never ask him to do something that would make him miserable. For him, she'd stay and risk a lifetime of imprisonment.

She would just fold her wings and fall, trusting him to catch her.

CHAPTER 15

THE WHOLE TRUTH AND NOTHING BUT

December 21st...

Stillwater versus Arabia Jensen...

"Order in the court!" The gavel fell with the triple-whack of authority—*bam bam bam*—and immediate silence swept the courtroom.

At almost six-feet, Judge Ramses cut an imposing figure in her heavy black robes. Ramses had a straight fall of long, lustrous black hair, which she wore up in a tight chignon. Her piercing onyx eyes stared into the souls of those before her. No one dared defy her.

Sphinx magic tolerated no falsehood, so an oath sworn to honesty became a binding geas upon those taking the stand.

For three tedious days, the prosecution trotted out witness after witness who provided testimony. Without fail, their testimony utterly damned Arabia, and cemented another piece into place in the case being built against her. Chase diligently cross-examined every person on the stand, in the desperate hope of uncovering something—anything—that might save her. As hard as he tried, he failed to turn up any surprising original tidbit that hadn't already been revealed in discovery. No new fact or shocking surprise of the sort that routinely presented late in the third act of a fictionalized courtroom drama upon which the dashing defense attorney turned the entire course of the case. Not that Chase, being a natural cynic, expected any such miracle, but he clung to a debilitating mix of hope and fear. During the long, sleepless nights that'd become his norm, he prayed to whatever god or goddess might be listening.

The fourth morning found Chase seated straight and tall at a weathered oak counter that served as the defendant's table. An open file folder lay before him, but before his tired eyes, the letters blurred and the words ran together. At his side, Arabia had taken to restless fidgeting that grated on his nerves. Chase quelled the urge to scold her as though she were a misbehaving child.

Officer Niles White was called as the first witness of the day. A slight man, unmemorable in all ways, the few thin strands of mousy-brown hair that he combed over constituted his most outstanding feature. Hand held in pledge, he solemnly swore the oath: "...the evidence I shall give shall be the whole truth and nothing but the truth."

Seamus Grayson rose from his seat at the prosecution table. Prior to speaking, the district attorney made a production of smoothing the front of his fine tweed suit. He adjusted his tie and fiddled with his cuff links until the whole courtroom hung on his first words with baited breath. Grudging admiration for the crafty old barrister curled in Chase's gut.

"Sir," Grayson said, spreading his Irish brogue on thicker than butter over warm country bread. "Please state your name and position."

White cleared his throat. He leaned in too close to the microphone and said, "Niles White." The microphone squealed, and he jerked away faster than a stork finding a snake in its nest. Wide-eyed, he stared at the device.

"Please continue," Grayson encouraged.

White hooked his finger into the starch-stiffened collar of his white dress shirt and pried it away, revealing the bobbing of his Adam's apple. "By position, you mean job title? Cause my position is seated..."

The jurors twittered.

Arabia snickered.

Judge Ramses scowled.

Silence fell.

Grayson bared his teeth. "I do mean your job title."

"I'm a police officer for the Stillwater Police Department," White said, nodding.

"And where were you on the evening of November 7th?" Grayson asked.

"I was working graveyard that evening. I always work graveyard. Normally I get to the precinct at nine, head out on patrol, and work until six a.m. But that particular evening, I came into work an hour early because the movie I'd been watching got cut short—"

"Objection, the witness is providing a narrative," Chase said.

"Sustained," Ramses returned. "The witness is directed to provide information relevant to the question being asked. Proceed."

"Officer White, do you feel that anything

unusual happened to you the evening of November 7th?" Grayson asked.

"Objection," Chase called out. "The prosecution is asking the witness to speculate."

"Sustained," said the judge. "District Attorney, rephrase the inquiry."

"In your own words, please describe the events of November 7th," Grayson said to the officer.

White got off to a faltering start. "Well, like I said, I got into work around eight and finished up some reports the chief had been on my case to finish. About 9:15 or so, I headed up to dispatch to let Shelly Godfrey—that's our dispatcher—know I was heading out on patrol. Only thing was, Shelly wasn't at her station."

"Did you locate Ms. Godfrey?" Grayson asked.

"Yes." White blushed something fierce. Beneath the harsh incandescent courtroom lights, sweat glistened on his balding scalp.

Grayson arched his brow. "Where did you find Ms. Godfrey?"

"They were in the records room," White said, stammering. "I walked in on them—"

"Them?" Grayson asked.

"Ms. Godfrey and Officer Bast," White said. "They were in a compromising position, so I shut the door as soon as I realized what they were up to. I swear, I didn't watch at all."

An orange halo flared about White—the sphinx's magical lie detector.

White flushed beet red. "I watched for a few seconds," he said, correcting his fib, and the glow faded.

The jury broke into uproarious laughter. Arabia slapped her knee, shoved her elbow into Chase's ribs, and doubled over. Despite his best effort, a smile tugged at the corners of his mouth. Chase bit it back.

Judge Ramses called for order and pounded her gavel multiple times before discipline was restored.

"Officer White, please finish recounting a brief summary of the events of the evening of November 7th and the early morning of the 8th, sticking strictly to facts," Grayson instructed.

"Strictly speaking, I shut the door and went to the dispatch station. It seemed impolite to interrupt, and I didn't want to leave the phones unmonitored, so I manned 'em for the rest of the evening."

"How many calls did you take that evening?"

"Whole bunch related to folks running about in the nude 'n' being engaged in obscene activities. It seemed like the whole goddamn town'd gone insane!" White threw up his hands. "Excuse my French."

"Define obscene."

If possible, the officer's complexion reddened even more. "People were having sex in public all over town. It was a fucking orgy. Excuse my French."

Grayson referenced a report on a clipboard. "Did you take a call on November 8th at 2:40 a.m.?"

"Yes."

"What was it in reference to?"

"A man called in an anonymous tip. He said the orgy was the result of malicious magic that'd been cast over the town by a ravenborn witch. He gave Arabia Jensen's name and home address, and then he hung up."

"Did you recognize the anonymous caller?"

White wiped perspiration off his brow. "No, not at the time."

"Was the call recorded?"

"No, it wasn't."

"And why was that?"

"I'm not too familiar with how the phones work. Somehow, I must've slipped up and turned off the recording system because none of the calls were recorded that evening."

"What did you do after you took the anonymous call?" Grayson asked.

"I drove my patrol car over to investigate. When I

arrived, I knocked on the front door. A man answered and granted me entry."

"Can you please identify the man?"

Chase braced for the answer. Beside him, Arabia squirmed.

"Yes, sir." White's glance skittered across the courtroom. "It was the defense attorney, Chase Baron."

Immediate salacious speculation arose from the jurors. Under the press of their gazes, Chase's wolf roiled but he kept a tight leash on his beast. Up until that moment, his relationship with Arabia had been private. Now it was on public record. Within seconds, Judge Ramses silenced the jury with a glare.

"Describe what happened next," Grayson said to the witness.

"All right." White flexed his shoulders in a subtle attempt at stretching. "Mr. Baron cooperated fully and answered my questions. He said Ms. Jensen was asleep in the bedroom. He gave me permission to look around the outer rooms as much as I needed to verify no crime had been committed—"

Arabia stiffened in abrupt shock.

Chase kept his head high and shoulders squared, but only with great difficulty. Guilt ate at him like a cancer. Oh, and shame... it sickened him. Here, he was an experienced attorney who, in his right mind, never should've allowed a search of private property without a warrant. His only defense was that he hadn't been of sound mind or body at the time. When he'd invited the police inside, Chase was still reeling under the influence of the Heart's Desire enchantment. It'd compromised his judgment.

The excuse provided cold comfort.

"Did you search the premises?" Grayson asked.

"Yes, I did," White said.

"And what did you find?"

"Magical components in the kitchen and written instructions for casting a love spell. There was enough there that I had probable cause, so I placed Ms. Jensen under arrest."

"Chase?" Arabia gasped.

He turned to face her. The awful betrayal and hurt confusion on her face cut him to the quick. He opened his mouth to explain... to apologize. But the entire courtroom was watching them, so he kept silent.

Luminous tears filled Arabia's eyes. "You're the reason I was arrested?"

CHAPTER 16

DEAD TO RIGHTS

Overwhelmed with emotion, Arabia allowed herself to be pushed along. In a twist of irony, Chase herded her to the tiny second-floor courthouse conference room he'd rescued her from the other night. She was no more thrilled to be here now than she'd been then; less so, especially in light of the devastating revelation that'd led to Chase requesting a recess from Judge Ramses.

The door shut with an ominous thunk. Arabia spun to confront him, but her vast hurt robbed her of words. She raised her hand to guard her heart. Beneath her palm, her chest heaved and her heart raced as though she'd been running a marathon.

He put his back to the door, crossed his arms,

and returned her regard. Seconds ticked past, but he didn't speak.

Arabia's patience ran out. She launched into a distressed demand, picking up where they'd left off in the courtroom. Thankfully, she'd had enough time to cool down just a tad. Even so, her voice quavered. "Did you really have me arrested?"

His face flushed. "I didn't have you arrested. Not on purpose. Not with premeditation—"

"Don't lawyer up!" Her temper flared and then snapped. "Did you or did you not invite the police into my house?"

"I did, but it's not like you're making it sound." Chase exhaled so his nostrils flared. Everything about him, from his posture to the sourness underlying his scent, pointed to his unraveling composure. Unmistakably, the alpha wolf had reached his limits.

Well, he thought he was pissed? He had *nothing* on her. Arabia asked, "How was it then?"

"There was a knock on the door at three a.m. I looked out and saw a police officer on the porch, so of course I answered."

"Answering the door to a cop doesn't mean you have to invite him in. The police can't be trusted—"

"So says the woman on felony trial." He

narrowed his eyes, which glowed bright enough to burn through her. "I had nothing to hide, so I had no reason not to ask him in out of the cold."

"It was my house. *Mine*—not yours. And you know me."

"Right. The woman who always has something to hide."

"I can't believe you did this. You, of all people. You're a lawyer. If anyone should know better than to surrender your Fourth Amendment rights, it's you."

Chase opened his mouth and snarled. He cocked his head, struggling to hold back whatever it was that he was really thinking. Eventually, he said, "Maybe I screwed up, but I wasn't in my right mind because of *that spell*."

"That spell relaxed your hang-ups. It didn't remove your ability to reason."

"It impaired my cognitive abilities. Stop trying to shift blame onto me for your misdeeds."

"So this is my fault, too? Just like everything else?"

"I call it as I see it."

She fumed. With each passing second, her anger mounted, ascending to new heights. "If you don't feel bad at all, then why didn't you tell me all this right from the beginning?"

"I never said I didn't feel bad."

"So you do feel guilty?"

"Feeling guilty and being guilty about something aren't always the same thing."

"Hiding the truth *is*. You told me that."

"So is twisting facts." Chase smiled, so smug, so superior, she wanted nothing more than to smack him.

"Why didn't you tell me the truth about how I got arrested?"

"Because I knew how you'd respond—just like this. I needed your cooperation." He spoke through clenched teeth, as though he made the confession with great difficulty.

"So you lied so you could manipulate me?"

"If that's not the pot calling the kettle black, I don't know what is. It's no worse than you did to me."

She couldn't argue that, so she hunched her shoulders. "It's no better, either."

With a look, he told her what he thought of her sullen reply. "Arabia, this whole mess from start to finish has been the result of your doing. You chose to cast that spell of your own free will. It's time for you to stop placing blame and making excuses. For the first time in your life, grow up and take responsibility for what you've done."

"You're right," Arabia winced. In a self-comforting gesture, she reached for the gold hair bead that anchored the small braid beneath her ear. She rubbed it between her fingers. Abruptly, the magnitude of her hypocrisy smacked her square over the head.

Chase didn't hear her. He continued to rant. "None of this is my fault. All I've done is try to help. I'm away from my home, my career, my pack. I dropped everything to be your attorney and the thanks I get? Lies, defiance... You're stubborn and self-destructive. You refuse to do anything that would help me get you out of this mess. Worse, you've sabotaged my ability to defend you!"

His shouted accusation blasted over Arabia. It delivered a devastating emotional blow. She recoiled from him, but her disgust was directed inward. At the same time, she was as confused as she was repulsed.

"How did I do that?" She raised pleading hands.

"For one, you refused the plea bargain I spent days finagling. It would have gotten you off with time served in exchange for a guilty plea and a fucking apology. But no, you couldn't swallow your damn pride long enough to admit you were wrong, could you?" Chase ran his hand through his hair in agitation. He looked drained and defeated. She recalled how wonderful it'd been to bring him joy when they made love at the courthouse, and it was equally devastating to understand that she'd caused him this despair.

"You're right. I'm sorry." Shame overcame her like a debilitating sickness. Nausea so bad she bent forward and gripped her stomach, fighting the urge to puke.

"Right about what?" Chase remained guarded, which only served to deepen her sadness. He didn't trust her at all, and that, too, was her fault.

So far, secrecy and trickery hadn't brought her anything but grief. She hadn't even said, "I love you" to Chase because he wouldn't believe her. And, if she was brutally honest with herself, why should he? Maybe, just maybe, it was time for her to come clean with the man she professed to adore above all others.

She took a deep breath and rushed to confess before she chickened out. "You're right about everything. I set this whole thing up from the very start. When I left those messages for Reidar, I knew he was out of the country and that he'd send you to check on me—"

"You really did all this to catch my attention?" Chase asked. Maybe it was her imagination running rampant, but did the man sound the least bit impressed?

"Yeah, pretty much. I planned the whole thing for months."

"I see." Chase folded his arms. His expression remained frustratingly inscrutable. She'd never been good at reading him once he got his guard up, but maybe that was because he never actually let it down.

"In my defense, I did try to seduce you. I only resorted to magic when that failed." Arabia crossed her arms also, hugging herself.

"Failed?" His jaw dropped. For a second, Chase frowned in obvious puzzlement but then his confusion cleared. "Do you mean when you sat on my lap and—"

"Yeah." She nodded vigorously.

Chase's voice spiked about three decibels. "You call *that* a failure? I was ready to rip your clothes off and take you right then and there."

"Then why didn't you?" She wrung her hands in a sudden fit of exasperation. Astonishment spiked through her.

"Because I wanted to talk about it first—to be

sure you understood what you wanted, and that you weren't rushing into something you'd regret later."

"Chase..." Arabia huffed. Oh for the love of Frigg's chariot cats! There were times when she just wanted to throttle the infuriating man! In a dark and twisted way, the whole thing was hilarious, but she doubted Chase would appreciate the humor. She swallowed a giggle and asked, "Are you telling me this whole thing could've been avoided if I'd just waited?"

He released a thin sigh. "It's bigger than just that."

"How so?" Arabia dared to slip closer to him. She crossed the space that separated them, reached out, and caught his fingers. He curled his hand about hers, big and warm.

A wry smile split the corner of Chase's mouth. "How much else is the result of misunderstandings that could've been avoided if we'd just talked?"

"I didn't think I'd ever see you laugh about this." She dared to grin.

"It's easier than crying." He shook his head. Deep blue sorrow flavored his basal scent, and she wanted to weep, too.

Uncomfortable silence filled the already claustrophobically small room. She started to feel hot and dizzy—the usual symptoms of an oncoming panic attack. Deliberately, she closed her eyes and concentrated on slowing her breathing. Chase's comforting presence helped soothe her nerves.

"How do we fix this?" Arabia asked, gazing up at him.

"I don't know. That's what I've been standing here trying to figure out. Officer White is the prosecution's key witness. He was shaky, at best, but still believable. When I go back in there to cross-examine him, I need something that will call his credibility into question or we're screwed." Chase ran his hand through his hair, messing up his precisely groomed locks.

"Have you investigated him? Maybe he's got some sick fetish—"

"Arabia, no."

"Why not? Everyone's got something—even you! There's that thing you like to do—"

"No." His scowl turned thunderous.

"No?" She quirked her lips and lifted her brow.

"I won't resort to dirty tactics to win. Maligning a police officer's reputation won't buy us any allies on the jury."

"Well, so long as you can sleep with your

conscience, I guess I'll learn to sleep on a prison frame bunk bed."

He stared at her, unwavering in his resolution.

She sighed and waved her hands in surrender. "Can you tell the DA that we changed our mind about the plea bargain? I swear, this time I'll sign it without a peep."

"Unfortunately, that's not an option anymore," Chase said with a wry grimace. "Seamus Grayson made it abundantly clear it was a limited-time offer."

"Which expired because of me?" She winced.

Chase was kind enough not to say, "I told you so."

"You could put me on the stand." Arabia braced, fully expecting him to refuse. They'd already had this argument many times over. Frankly, she was at a total loss and desperate for ideas. Maybe now that they were finally communicating, they could put their heads together and formulate an actual plan.

"No."

Arabia flushed on a surge of anger. "No? You flat-out refuse to even discuss it?"

Chase snapped straight back to sternness. "Correct. No good can come of you testifying. I've heard your side of the story. Whether you like it or not, it's damning. As your lawyer, I refuse to allow you to incriminate yourself." All trace of humor vanished from his face, now set in a stony mask. He obviously expected her to fight him on it.

"Okay." Arabia clenched her teeth and tucked her chin. She didn't like it, but she resolved not to argue. But it stung. Oh, how it hurt.

"Okay?" He blinked.

"I trust your judgment. Even though it might not seem like it, I don't want to go to prison. I want to start helping you defend me, so if you say I can't testify, then I won't testify."

Chase raised their joined hands, drawing attention to her white-knuckled grip. The tightness in her joints, though, paled in comparison to the constriction in her chest. When he rubbed his thumb over her fingers, she trembled.

"Why does that upset you so much?" Chase dropped his volume to only slightly above a husky whisper. He'd picked up on how much it mattered to her and that scared her to death.

Arabia opened her mouth but no sound emerged. She shook her head, waging an internal war. She had a secret eating at her insides. The stress of keeping it was destroying her, but she lacked the courage necessary to tell him.

"Arabia? You know whatever it is, you can tell me."

She gulped, swallowing around the lump in her throat. His gentleness somehow made opening up to him more difficult, rather than less. Call it an antagonist mindset thanks to a lifetime of verbal dueling and mind games they'd shared. But when she took a good hard look at herself, this wasn't who she wanted to be anymore. This wasn't any good for *them*. To conquer her fear, she needed to open herself up and risk rejection. What was the worst that could happen?

He could accuse her of lying.

"I wanted to testify because of Judge Ramses's truth power," she blurted out.

He knit his brow. "I'm not sure I follow."

"Look, you don't believe half of what I say—"

"That's not true."

She looked at him.

"Okay, but not half." Chase's mouth split in a sheepish smile. "I question maybe a third of what you tell me, but do you blame me?"

"No." She gave a quick shake of her head. "I don't, and I also don't have anyone else to blame but that."

"So you figured you could say whatever it is you've been keeping from me while under the influence of the sphinx's magic and I'd have to believe you?"

She nodded.

Chase stroked his fingers along her jawline and lifted her chin, forcing her to meet his gaze. "Say what you want to say. You have my word, I'll trust you."

Unshed tears stung her eyes. A hangman's noose constricted her throat. She blinked repeatedly and bit her lips. "I love you."

Chase's expression remained stoic, and his lack of reaction scared her to death. It'd been terrifying to put herself out there. Totally and truly vulnerable. But now that she'd begun, she mustn't stop.

"I only cast that stupid love spell because I couldn't stand to live another day without you." She rushed the confession for fear she'd change her mind. "I swear by our gods, I never meant to harm you or force you to act against your will. The magic was only supposed to free you from your doubts and fears and hang-ups. You've gotta admit, you've got an awful lot of those."

She waited a beat, but still he didn't say anything. Wry cynicism washed over her. Poor guy. He'd promised not to call her a liar, tying his own hands.

"I knew this was a mistake." Arabia gave a bitter laugh and turned her face aside. It hurt too much to face him. Trauma reduced her to a trembling mess—she shook from head to toe.

"Arabia." He reached for her but a hard, perfunctory knock on the door of the conference room interrupted whatever else he'd meant to say.

In unison, they turned toward the entrance as the door swung inward, revealing one of the uniformed courthouse guards. He held up a cordless phone. "Mr. Baron, I'm sorry to interrupt, but you have a call. The woman said it's urgent."

"I had my phone on silent for court." Chase shot an apologetic look at Arabia. She jerked her chin, telling him to take the call. Truth be told, she welcomed the interruption if it bought her even a few minutes to recover her composure.

"Thank you." Chase advanced a step and accepted the device. He waited until the guard left before he addressed the receiver. "Hello?"

The mysterious caller talked fast. Chase listened and asked the occasional ambiguous question like "Are you sure?" and "Did you obtain the evidence?"

Arabia listened on pins and needles, each passing moment an added torture. As much as drama and suspense appealed to her ravenborn nature, she decided she didn't much care to be on the receiving end.

When Chase finally hung up, he flashed a wide wolf's smile—lots of teeth. A dangerous gleam shone in his feral gaze. So damn handsome he stole her breath away and her heart jumpstarted within her breast.

"What is it?" she asked.

"We've got them!" Chase smashed his fist against his open palm. "Dead to rights."

CHAPTER 17

A HARD BARGAIN

Bookshelves lined every square inch of the justice's chambers. A hot, dry odor pervaded the room—a mix like old books and ancient knowledge. It tickled the insides of Chase's nose, leaving him fending off a perpetual sneeze. Prior to this trial, he would've guessed a sphinx would smell like a lion, not an enigma.

He considered himself schooled.

Judge Ramses presided from behind an oak Harvard Scholars Desk with a leather inlay top. There were chairs for guests, but Chase and Grayson both remained on their feet as an invitation to take a seat hadn't been extended.

"Would you care to explain yourself now, Mr. Baron?" Judge Ramses directed a severe stare straight at Chase. She conveyed the impression of immense annoyance, but he tried not to take it personally. The sphinx personified perpetual aggravation in its entirety.

Grayson, for his part, radiated Machiavellian cunning. The wily wolf observed everything but said nothing, too experienced to succumb to impatience.

"I have new evidence to introduce. I've uncovered the identity of the caller who phoned in the anonymous tip that brought Officer White to my client's residence." Chase smoothly presented a file folder to the judge who accepted it. While she scanned the top page, Grayson scowled and pursed his lips.

Ramses glanced up. She addressed Chase. "Proceed."

"The caller was Damian Charming, a detective with the Stillwater Police Department. Lieutenant Charming was Ms. Jensen's would-be suitor at one point. When his advances were rejected, he took to stalking my client. I've obtained photographs and recordings that prove that Officer Charming used police surveillance equipment to monitor Ms. Jensen's residence. He did so without a warrant and in violation of my client's Fourth Amendment rights."

"What proof do we have the surveillance equipment wasn't planted to frame Detective Charming?" Grayson asked.

"I figured you'd suggest that." Chase worked his jaws in anger. Even though it wasn't personal, the suggestion that he'd engage in unethical behavior offended him. "That's why I contacted an old friend of mine in the FBPI and asked them to secure the scene."

The Federal Bureau of Paranormal Investigation operated under the umbrella of the FBI. The subsidiary department specialized in probing criminal matters that violated national regulations, including violations by state law enforcement agencies.

Grayson cleared his throat. "Regardless of whether Detective Charming conducted himself in an unprofessional—"

"Illegal—" Chase snapped.

"Manner," Grayson kept going, "this doesn't change anything. Officer White had no knowledge regarding the identity of the anonymous caller. He testified under oath, so unless you're challenging the veracity of the sphinx's truth aura, none of this is relevant."

"Thank you, Mister District Attorney, but I'll

determine what's relevant." Judge Ramses aimed her fearsome regard at Seamus.

"Of course, Your Honor. I intended no disrespect." Grayson bowed his head, but even a skilled old thespian like the district attorney couldn't conceal his mounting aggravation.

The judge gestured to Chase. "Mr. Baron?"

"When Officer White was asked if he knew the identity of the caller, his exact words were, 'No, not at this time.' When I cross-examine him, I intend to ask Officer White when he realized the true identity of the anonymous caller. I won't be surprised to discover that it was before he gave testimony during discovery. The prosecution's key witness withheld essential evidence to protect a fellow officer's corruption. Maybe White was only acting out of a sense of loyalty to his fellow officer, but it calls his integrity into question. What other illegal or immoral activities has he engaged in?"

The atmosphere grew severe and volatile.

Judge Ramses brewed like a gathering storm. Grayson looked as though he'd been weaned on a pickle. Chase had the DA over a barrel, and Seamus knew it. For his part, Chase maintained a stoic demeanor. He kept his triumph under tight wraps. This thing wasn't won yet. He had enough to call the legality of the defense's case into question, but doing so meant exposing police corruption to the public eye. When scandals of this nature erupted, there was no telling how far the consequences might reach... or how high.

Chase glanced at the judge. Abruptly, he got good and nervous.

"This is your mess, Mr. Grayson. How do you intend to handle it?" Ramses asked, tapping her finger.

"What do you want—a mistrial?" Grayson asked.

"No." Chase shook his head. A mistrial meant the prosecution would retain the ability to compile more evidence and file charges again in the future. He refused to risk that. He needed to ensure Arabia's immediate and long-term freedom.

"Then what?" Grayson asked.

"We'll accept that plea bargain you offered prior to the trial starting. In exchange for an admission of guilt and time served, Ms. Jensen goes free."

"Why would you put us through all this, only to change your mind now?" Grayson ended the inquiry on a hiss. Anger worked his face—a violent tic tugged at the corner of his mouth.

"We had some issues to work out."

"Fine," Grayson bit off. "Do I have your guarantee

the matter with the FBPI will be resolved quickly and quietly?"

"One call and I can have the investigation closed," Chase said.

Grayson nodded. "I'll be adding a non-disclosure clause requiring you and your client to keep details of the case and the agreement confidential."

"Agreed." Chase hesitated and then flashed a feral smile. "Remove the apology clause while you're making revisions."

Chase would be damned before Arabia was forced to say she was sorry to a man like Seamus Grayson. The alpha of the Baron Pack refused to subject his future mate to that humiliation. If the ravenborn had apologies to make, she could undertake those privately... and on her own terms.

Grayson's throat worked as though a fine bone had gotten stuck—one of the hazards of eating crow. But eventually he stuck out his hand and coughed up, "Done."

They shook on it.

"I have a final condition of my own, Mr. Baron," Judge Ramses interrupted in an imperious tone.

The two men started and faced the judge.

"Once the paperwork is signed and Ms. Jensen is free, I want both you and your client to leave

Stillwater and never return. The two of you and your vaudeville romance have turned my quiet little home on its ear. If I don't ever see either of you again in this lifetime, it'll be too soon."

"Yes, ma'am," Chase agreed, face burning. "You have my word."

CHAPTER 18

SIDE-SEAT DRIVER

Thick sheets of rain sluiced across the front window. Beads danced and shimmied, vibrating until they merged into larger droplets, which then bled into long, fast streaks that raced toward the edges of the glass. The windshield wipers labored, even on their highest setting, working to keep the glass clear, but it was coming down heavy enough to cover them again in a matter of seconds.

Arabia crossed her arms over her chest and hunched in the reclined front passenger seat. She stared straight ahead, gazing into darkness while the luxury sedan negotiated the winding mountainous road. A Canadian comedy station droned on the satellite radio, but Chase had the volume turned so low it was barely audible over the background din of the vehicle and storm. Their journey would eventually take them down out of the Sierra Nevada Mountains. Once they reached the Central Valley, they'd head south toward Los Angeles.

"Are you cold?" Chase reached for the climate controls and bumped it up a notch without waiting for her response. He'd been like this—overly solicitous and maddeningly presumptive—for the last several hours. The ink hadn't even dried on the plea bargain before he'd whisked her into his car, acting as though her welfare depended on leaving that courthouse behind her. And he was right... if she never saw that place again, it would be too soon.

"I'm fine. Thanks." She sighed. *Hardness.* She envisioned a protective shell surrounding her heart and strove to transform thought into energy.

Chase nodded and didn't say anything else, but the weight of his gaze slid across her, wary and appraising at the same time. He kept his impenetrable guard up. She couldn't decide whether his discomfort had been stymied from not knowing what to say to her or a reluctance to speak his mind. Most likely, it was the latter. As a rule, Chase Baron considered and weighed every word before he voiced it. Her polar opposite—too bad they weren't bears.

Life would be a lot simpler with a heavy meal and a hibernation cycle between arguments.

Lightning arced somewhere in the clouds overhead; thunder followed seconds later, and the radio crackled. The commotion jarred Arabia from her stupor. She turned off the talk show and tapped the heat controls, nudging it down.

"I texted my mother," Arabia volunteered because she couldn't abide silence. Consider it a flaw of her raven nature. Or call a spade a spade—the writhing insecurity in her gut rendered even short-term peace of mind impossible for her.

"Yeah? I'll bet she's thrilled to hear you're coming home."

"She's already making plans." Arabia bobbed her head so her bangs swung toward her face. Her incarceration had ruined the definition of her Cleopatra-bob to the point where she was thinking of growing it out. Maybe it was time to go for a whole new look.

"You don't sound thrilled." Chase kept his inflection perfectly neutral. She cast a sharp glance toward him anyway, seeking a hint of what he was really feeling, but his expression was impenetrable.

"I'm not."

He tightened his grip on the steering wheel. "Why not?"

"Why am I not thrilled over being taken back to my conspiracy in shame? Gee, let me think about that. Hmm..." She pressed her fingertip to the side of her chin.

"What the others make of your return is entirely dependent on what you tell them. I've seen your brother twist the retelling of an utter defeat into a tale of triumph."

She flashed a wry smile. "My mother always says, 'Reidar could come out of an outhouse explosion looking shinier than a new penny and—'"

"—and smelling like a bed of roses," Chase finished.

They traded bright grins.

Abruptly, Arabia's thoughts veered off course, following a wild tangent. Before she'd even formulated a conclusion, she heard herself ask, "What's going to happen with Damian Charming?"

Chase blinked and lost his smile.

"If you think I haven't noticed that you're evading the subject, think again." The first time she asked, he hadn't answered. The second, he changed the subject.

"The police are looking for him." Chase clipped his words.

"Stop stonewalling. The terms of the plea bargain mean he can't ever be charged and tried for stalking, don't they?" It'd taken her a couple hours to figure that out. She would've deduced it faster, but things had been nonstop since the second she was officially released. Chase hadn't given her a spare minute to reflect.

"I'm not stonewalling and that's correct," Chase replied in a terse tone. He wore a thin veil of humanity this night. His wolf lurked close to the surface. For the most part, he kept the beast hidden but not entirely. For one thing, the colored parts of his eyes wholly eclipsed the whites. She doubted he was even aware of the telling slipup, which showed just how deeply this had affected him. More than he wanted to let on, she was sure.

"I can't even file a restraining order against him, can I? I can't tell the police or a different judge why I'd need one." *That* scared her, although maybe it was senseless fear.

Charming hadn't done anything to her directly. Well, other than break into her home, use sophisticated surveillance equipment to monitor her, and then gotten her arrested... She shuddered to consider what the deranged psycho might've done if they'd actually dated more than once. The man might be a powerful warlock and a trained police officer in possession of a firearm, but he'd never threatened to harm her. Maybe she was being silly getting worked up over what was probably a baseless threat.

"You don't need a restraining order." Chase phrased it as a definitive fact. No argument allowed. He'd been doing a lot of *that*, too, since her release. Dogmatic, authoritarian, unilateral decrees. For instance, he hadn't bothered to ask her whether she wanted to leave Stillwater.

They'd dropped by her house so she could pack a couple bags, and he stood over her the whole time as though convinced she'd take off if he turned his back. That'd been the only stop on their way out of town. According to Chase, the rest of her belongings, including her car, would be "sent for."

"I don't?" Arabia tossed her hair since she lacked feathers to ruffle at the moment. Her disinclination to argue came to an abrupt end.

"No, you don't."

"Do you think he'll just stop stalking me? Lose interest because I left town?" She twisted in her seat to face him fully.

He spared her a two-second stare. "You don't need a restraining order because, if Damian Charming ever comes anywhere near you again, I'm going to kill him."

"Oh." The wind gusted from her lungs, and, quite involuntarily, she grinned. "I love it when you get all *grrr*-growly!"

"I'm serious." He said it as a lament, but she managed to coach a small smile from him anyway. Humor didn't last long, though, for either of them.

"I know you are, but it's not fair." Arabia settled her hand on the passenger side door beside the electronic window control. She tapped her fingers and considered lowering it.

"What's not fair?" Chase took his attention off the road again to steal another sideways glance.

"You always get stuck having to rescue me. We go straight from one mess to the next without a break. I'm the ultimate damsel in distress." Arabia sighed. She'd always thought of herself as a self-rescuing princess, but recent events had taken some of the tint off her rose-colored glasses.

"I like being your hero." He smiled as he said it and came as close to purring as a wolf possibly could. It made her giggle, despite the gloomy funk hanging over her.

Sadness tempered her joy. Her valiant wolf protector might've won her freedom, but the plea bargain hadn't solved all their problems. Not by a long shot. She'd been a fool to think otherwise, even for a second. The Heart's Desire spell hadn't resolved any of her and Chase's real issues. Once the magic faded, their problems returned tenfold. Those same doubts and fears that'd kept them apart their entire adult lives divided them now. But even those weren't insurmountable. There was one irreconcilable difference, though, that no amount of talking could fix... and it just broke her heart.

She loved Chase, but he didn't love her.

Arabia settled her forearm on the door panel, resting her hand beside the power button for the window. In agitation, she continued to tap her fingers against the hard resin and gave serious consideration to releasing her seat belt. In the time it took to roll down the window, she could shift, altering her clothing with her, and take flight. The prospect of flying into a storm scared her, but not half as much staying to hear what Chase might say to her.

"Don't. Please don't run from me." Chase caught her wrist in an ironclad grip. Startled, she glanced down. His hand, like his voice, shook.

"What makes you think—" She started to lie but

then cut herself short. No more deception. He deserved better. "Maybe leaving is the right thing to do. When I think about all the trouble I caused... and it's still not over. Charming is still out there."

"I told you—Charming is a dead man. Be honest. That's not the real reason you're thinking about running."

"You're right. I'm ready to leave because I'm a coward. But that doesn't automatically make it the wrong thing to do." She drew in a sharp breath and tugged at her arm, trying to free herself. "Please."

"I can't let go." He tightened his hold.

"It'll be easier this way."

"Easier for who? You said you loved me." His voice was pitched low and tight, thick with powerful passion.

"I do... and you didn't say it back." She choked on a sob. It took everything she had to suppress the tears. She kept an ocean of grief stopped up behind a paper-thin dam.

"Oh." Chase winced.

Dead silence. Outside the shelter of the vehicle, the weather worsened. The driving rain turned to white streaks that shot horizontally out of the dark sky. Snow flurries struck the front windshield, splattering like icy bugs, before the high-powered wipers swiped them aside. The headlights lit up the reflectors on the guardrail, but blackness yawned beyond. Then, all of a sudden, they both started talking at the same time.

"Chase, I don't want you to lie to me—"

"Arabia, I know I mishandled this whole thing—"

"Just to make me feel better." She held up a staying hand, but he had his attention focused on the road.

"I had to focus on your legal defense."

"It's okay. You shouldn't have to apologize for not feeling the way I do." She licked her lips, which were chapped and dry.

"I love you, too." Chase murmured. "With all my heart."

Her breath hitched. Every muscle in her body bunched the same as when she readied for flight. In the grip of wild hope and fear, she twisted around to stare at Chase's granite profile. Excitement surged through her. She needed to grab the man and kiss him silly. A thin thread of common sense stopped her from pursuing the impulsive course that would've certainly caused a car wreck.

"You're my mate. I must've known that for years on some level, but I refused to acknowledge it. It's tearing me apart knowing that you went through all this because you were too scared to tell me how you really felt."

"Chase, I'm the one to blame. This whole mess was my fault."

"I wasn't worthy of your trust, and in that, I failed you. I'm sorry."

"Tell you what—I'll make you a deal." Arabia lifted her arm, raising his hand as well. She bent and pressed a soft kiss against the back of his forearm, savoring his hot skin and coarse hair beneath her lips.

"What's that?" He exhaled, and the tautness bled from his athletic frame. He caught her hand, palm to palm, and interlaced their fingers. Sweet, but she craved spicy. A naughty impulse swept her.

"I'll forgive you..." She released her seat belt and twisted to face him, practically sitting on the center console that divided the bucket seats. She settled her hand atop Chase's thigh. An appreciative purr rumbled in her throat, and she pressed her fingers into the compact muscles.

"Ah, Arabia..." Chase inhaled through clenched teeth. He returned both hands to the ten and two o'clock positions on the steering wheel in a valiant attempt to respect proper driving safety.

"Yes, Chase?" Arabia asked in the voice of exaggerated innocence. She reached higher and cupped her palm to his crotch. His cock awaited her —stiff and stony beneath the fine wool.

"That's probably not a good idea." Chase rumbled the warning. "Ah, what were you saying about forgiving me?"

"I wasn't saying. I mean it. I want you to know I'm not holding a grudge."

"No conditions? We're not going to negotiate?" He stole a sharp glance before returning his attention to the road. The intelligence in his gaze amazed her. How did the man even have enough blood left in his head to think, let alone reason? She must not be doing this right.

"Negotiating would be pointless. You're going to forgive me. You always do." A wicked little smile curved her lips. She squeezed his groin, massaging him gently through the fine wool of his trousers.

A lusty groan tore from his throat. "Stop. You've gotta stop."

"But I'm helping you drive."

"How do you figure that?" He chuckled and altered his position, arching into her caress like a great cat beast begging for pets. Of course, she wasn't fooled for a second. Her Big Bad Wolf radiated a palpable aura of danger. She was playing with fire, but she wasn't afraid of getting burned.

"I'm working the stick shift." She licked her lips. Temptation pulled at her, and she desperately wanted to lower his zipper. Even she had the good sense to realize that'd be suicide at this speed, in these conditions. Better wait until he could pull off the highway at the next opportunity.

She started to suggest as much when the high beams of another car flooded their rear window. With a fearful start, she snatched her hand back and twisted to look over her shoulder. Based on how its headlights shone down into the sedan's interior, it had to be a truck or a sports utility vehicle. The roar of its engine droned over the storm, and their tailgater blasted his horn.

"Asshole," Chase snarled and adjusted his rear view mirror so the reflected light wouldn't blind him.

The SUV suddenly accelerated, bearing down on top of them

"They're going to hit us!" Arabia screamed the warning.

Swearing, Chase stomped down on the accelerator. They sped up, but not fast enough. The SUV plowed into them with a solid thunk that propelled the sedan forward. A gap opened between the two vehicles again.

"The asshole is trying to run us off the road."

Chase smashed the pedal to the metal, maintaining their lead. The SUV hung on their rear bumper with demonic determination.

"It's Damian Charming." Absolute conviction seized Arabia. Without a shred of solid evidence, she *knew* in her gut that the warlock was following them.

"We're entering a curve—at this speed, we'll crash," Chase said, depressing the control to lower the passenger side window. Frigid air blasted through the interior of the sedan.

"What are you doing?" Arabia shouted over the noise of the wind.

"Fly!" Chase shoved her toward the open window.

For what may've been the first time in her life, Arabia obeyed without hesitation or protest. She shifted straight into her raven form, taking her clothing with her, and shot through into the storm.

Gale force winds snatched her up and carried her away, twisting and tumbling, out of control. The wind battered her around like a cat toying with live prey. It tossed her high and plunged her low.

Far below, Chase's sedan crashed through the barricade and careened down the heavily forested mountain slope.

CHAPTER 19

GRAND THEFT BAUBLE

Chase came to in a red haze—groggy and disoriented —that seared through his mind. Everything hurt, even his hair follicles, the sort of epic injury that bards wrote sagas about. He felt like he'd downed an entire bottle of Dwarven spirits and gone rounds with an ice giant. On the upside, it meant he was still alive. On the down, he doubted anyone would be writing any songs about his misadventure anytime soon.

Heat washed over his skin. It crackled and popped. When he raised his arm to shield his face, the lively flames singed the hair on the back of his neck. Smoke flooded his nostrils.

The car was on fire.

Struggling to orient himself, Chase drew in a

deep breath and immediately regretted it. Smolder flooded his lungs, and painful coughing wracked his body. The thick smoke reduced visibility to a matter of inches. A large, amorphous *thing*—threatening in its size and proximity and his inability to immediately identify it—hovered only a few inches from his face. Tightness pressed against his chest and constricted his movements.

Trapped in an overturned, burning vehicle, his circumstances had just skipped from bad to worse. Without warning, the shapeless object billowed and quivered like a spineless puffer fish. Its edge thwacked his chin.

Adrenaline surged through Chase, and his wolf surged to dominance. A growl rumbled his chest, his wolf's primitive and instinctive reaction to the imminent threat. He punched straight through the deployed air bag, which burst with a flatulent sound. Hitting the solid steering column was the same as hitting a wall. He bloodied his knuckles and agony lanced through his hand when what must've been a dozen small bones fractured. The impact jammed his entire arm all the way to his shoulder.

"Fuck!" The shout exploded from Chase. He clutched his injured limb to his chest, suffering through the discomfort until his augmented werewolf healing kicked in. The whole thing cleared his befuddlement right up.

He clenched his fists and flipped them open, performing a partial shift of his hands. His bones crunched and remolded, the broken ones healing in the process. Dark gray fur erupted across his skin. Deadly sharp claws erupted from the tips of his fingers, which he used to slice through the seatbelt that was holding him in the driver's seat.

The second he cut himself free, he dropped a couple of feet and smashed his chest against the steering column, bruising his entire ribcage. If karma was somehow at play here, the spirit of his car was seriously pissed at him.

Righting himself, Chase folded his considerable bulk almost in half to turn within the cramped interior. The trunk of a tree barricaded the shattered front windshield. In the backseat, the conflagration flared suddenly. Arms of flame reached into the passenger seat, barring his path through the open window. He ducked his head to protect his face from the inferno. Twisting, Chase kicked out the driver's side window with his heel and reverse-crawled through the opening.

The moment he cleared the burning vehicle, a welcome gale of cold air carrying swirling snowflakes in its grasp gusted over him. Chase sucked in a deep breath of refreshing air.

Chase lurched upright and stumbled away from the blazing car. His suit jacket was on fire. Flames fed on the sleeve, emitting a column of smoke, and blistered his skin. While he ran, he shed his coat and ripped off his shirt.

A brilliant flash of heat and light flared at his back; the sonic boom followed a second later. The force of the explosion knocked him off his feet. Chase face-planted and the flare washed over him, searing his bare back. A projectile smashed into the trunk of a pine tree a few feet away and shattered in a rain of shrapnel. He hugged the frozen earth until the firestorm receded, and only then did he raise his head.

He faced down a steep slope somewhere on the side of the mountain. Overhead, the storm clouds blocked the moon and stars. The unrelenting wind lashed his head and shoulders. Remnants of the burning vehicle emanated an eerie orange radiance. Murky shadows snuck through the thick stands of pine trees that surrounded him on all sides.

Carefully, Chase climbed to his feet and took a step, testing the terrain. The earth was slick and icy —no nice, clean snowpack. With his first step, the sole of his shoe hit a patch of treacherous black ice. His leg slid sideways. He pulled back to stop from going down. Well, that decided it—four legs would be safer and faster than two. He kicked off his shoes, shed his boxers and pants, and gathered his strength.

A raucous craw fell from above. Seconds later, a pitch-black raven swooped out of the sky and alighted on a jagged stump. Vast relief washed through Chase that Arabia was unharmed. Her spectacular escape from the speeding sedan had been hazardous, especially given the stormy conditions.

"Thank the gods." He reached out, using the side of his clawed hand to stroke her sleek head. She arched into his touch, crooning with affection.

"Are you okay?" Arabia asked in her avian-voice.

"Yeah, I'm all right." A plethora of cuts, burns, and bruises covered his body, but he'd already begun to heal. Later, he'd be starving but for now, his concern centered on survival. Anger roiled in his gut. His wolf clung to it with locked jaws like a juicy bone, unwilling to let go.

"It *is* Damian. He's coming." Arabia's head crest stood stiff and fully erect, signaling her agitation.

"Good." Chase figured the odds were in his favor against Damian Charming. A human, magic-user or not, would be at a disadvantage in this terrain, in the dark, and against a wolf.

"Chase, he's summoned hellhounds to track you. You have to run!"

"Hellhounds?"

On cue, a brassy yowl punctured the stormy night; a second unearthly call echoed the first. Both originated from above, at some point higher on the mountainside. They sounded like something straight out of a Wes Craven movie, and it riled up his wolf in the worst way possible. A growl rumbled in the depths of his chest, and his primal instincts screamed —*fight, rend, kill.*

"Yes, big, nasty, ugly-ass hounds from hell. He has two of them!" Arabia flapped her wings but clung to her perch with her talons.

That gave him pause to consider, but only for a moment. He refused to flee from the psychotic asshole that had caused Arabia so much misery. Besides, running only delayed the inevitable. As a predator, he understood the nature of the hunt. Charming would keep coming after Arabia, and next time, his ambush might succeed. No, the warlock had to die, and Chase meant to do the killing.

"I'm not running." He wanted to ask questions, to see if he could coax more useful information out of her, but he didn't have time. Those so-called hellhounds were less than a quarter mile distant and closing fast.

Arabia emitted a frightened squawk. "Chase, don't be stupid! This is no time to be a hero. You're injured and outnumbered."

"No." Chase gathered his strength and initiated a shift to his wolf form. Energy flowed across his skin, and his gaze cast an incandescent radiance. His physical transformation began, but at half his usual pace and it hurt way more than usual.

Fur covered his skin. Bones snapped and cartilage crunched as his body pushed and pulled this way and that. His ears closed to points and migrated to the top of his skull, and his jaws distended to a snout.

Arabia got real quiet. She tilted her head to the side, and then she said, in that universal tone of female disapproval, "Fine, I'll do what I can to help. Do you see those crossed trees over there?"

He looked to where she pointed her beak. The bonfire had burned down slightly, but a fat smokestack rose from it. Within the fiery halo, a pair of pines formed a lopsided-X. From the looks of it, one of the trees was dead and propped against the other. It looked ready to topple—miraculous that it hadn't fallen already. He immediately grasped her intent.

"Yeah, I see them." Those would be the last words he spoke—was physically capable of speaking. Razor-sharp canines ruptured from his gums, and he swiftly passed the midway point between human and beast, the classic monster-movie wolfman. His arms altered to front legs, and his claw-like hands became paws. Chase dropped to all fours and shook his entire body, working the final kinks out of his spine and tail. As a wolf, he had dark gray fur, and his stature was far larger than that of a common lupine.

"Lure them through there." Arabia took flight without waiting for his answer. Chase didn't have time to track her trajectory. The forest reverberated with the sharp cracks of broken branches.

Chase gathered himself to sprint. Bursting with belligerence, he held on the mark, waiting for the enemy to make their appearance.

A pair of huge, unnatural creatures surged into the clearing. Chase agreed with Arabia's assessment of their appearance—ugly bastards—but to him they seemed more like pigs than hounds. Each beast had three glowing beady eyes and crinkled snouts set within broad faces. A pair of wicked curved tusks jutted from their lower jaws. Bearlike builds—barrel-shaped torsos and short, thick limbs. Instead of fur, they had ashen hides covered in shiny scales. A row of spines ran down the middle of their backs, ending in a stubby tail.

The gale-force wind descended from the sky, beating at them with invisible fists. It howled louder than the beasts, and whipped the bonfire to new heights. A tower of sparks flared forth.

Overhead, a raven screamed.

The hounds hesitated, noticed him, and altered their bearing. The larger of the hellhounds let loose a baying-cry and charged straight at Chase. Its companion followed three strides behind.

Chase turned tail. He dug his claws into the frozen ground and poured on a burst of speed. He passed between the trunks of the leaning trees. Ahead, a dense copse of undergrowth barred his path. Breaking through it would slow him down, leaving his back exposed. Chase dug in his claws and went into a skid, performing a full about-face. He dropped into a fighting stance, head held low to protect his throat.

A swirling whirlwind reached out of the storm and whacked against the rotted trunk of the dead timber. With a tremendous crack, the pine tree fell.

The lead hound cleared the passage unscathed. The thick trunk smashed over the second beast's back. Bones crunched. An agonized squeal erupted from the beast and ended abruptly

Score one for the good guys.

The death of its companion didn't slow the leader. The hound's trio of eyes shone with malice, and hot puffs of acrid breath poured from its snout. The sulfuric scent supported Arabia's conclusion that the beast was hell-spawned. Deep, jagged scars covered the gray hide. It bore down on Chase, its cloven hooves ripping up the rocky soil. The hound angled its ebony tusks and stabbed at the wolf.

He waited until the last second and then leapt aside. The glistening tusks passed near enough to shave the fur off his shoulder. As the hound thundered past, Chase sprang and descended on the beast's back. He latched on with fangs and claws. The scaly hide proved tougher than it appeared. His attack opened long, shallow slashes.

The hellhound proved strong and shockingly swift, especially for a beast of its bulk. It screeched and bucked, throwing Chase off. He twisted and landed on his feet, bracing for another attack. Before he oriented himself, the hound descended on him again.

It stabbed a curved tusk straight at his face. Chase dodged, once again evading impalement but only by a matter of inches. Breathing hard, he retreated and leapt over the downed tree.

The moment he dropped out of sight, he hunched down and tucked himself against the side of the trunk. Baying and the tromping of its hooves marked the hound's charge. As expected, it soared directly overhead.

Teeth bared, Chase attacked from behind. This time, he aimed low. Before the hellhound sensed he was there, he locked his jaws on the back of its rear leg. His fangs sank deep, penetrating the tough hide, and embedded in the underlying sinew. The hound's flesh tasted like spoiled meat.

The hound screeched and jumped. Chase lunged, throwing all his weight behind the motion, and ripped out its hamstring. He came away with a huge hunk of skin and muscle. Blood gushed from the wound.

With an infuriated caterwaul, the hound swung around, moving on its three good legs. It dragged its injured limb and stabbed with its tusks at the space Chase had occupied seconds before.

Circling behind, Chase drove for the hound's other rear leg. With his fangs, he severed the large tendon. Crippled, the beast's hindquarters went out from under it. Squealing, it collapsed into a quivering heap.

Filled with scorn, Chase gave a wolf's sneer. His lips curled over his teeth. He stepped in and finished off the hound, ripping out its throat. Afterward, he spat out the foul-tasting flesh. Tilting back his head, Chase roared in triumph, mightier than a lion, fiercer than a tiger.

"Oh, bravo! That was marvelous!" The man's voice was cultured, and he had an exotic accent. He accentuated his mockery with a slow, loud clap.

Chase pivoted toward the sound. He recognized Damian Charming from photographs Laura had provided. The warlock had a tall, powerful build. Long, straight black hair fell to his jawline. His bright gold eyes burned like living flames, and it seriously irritated the fuck out of Chase to have to acknowledge that if looks could kill, the warlock would have to register as a lethal weapon.

Yeah, the guy was *that* handsome.

Curiosity led Chase to undertake another shift in reverse of the last. He progressed from a wolf to a wolf-man hybrid, and halted the transition after he'd recovered the ability to speak.

"You think this is funny?" Chase took umbrage

over the warlock's smirk. The bastard personified smugness.

"Well, no. Not really. On the whole, I'm far from amused." Damian cocked his head and raised his hands, drawing attention to the chunky, square silver rings he wore on each finger. The jewelry shone with the radiance of enchantment.

Double silver brass knuckles—Chase possessed the good sense to be wary.

"What the hell is wrong with you?" Chase demanded. Nothing about Charming struck him as quite right. He couldn't believe he was even thinking it, but the guy seemed too sane to be an obsessed stalker... and way too dangerous to attack without due consideration.

"What's wrong with me?" Damian asked with parted lips. He raised an offended hand to his chest.

"Yeah, you. Why are you stalking my woman?" Chase huffed. A snarl curled in his throat. Maybe it'd been a mistake to delay. He ought to attack and just get the inevitable over with.

"Your woman?" Damian rocked back on his heels in apparent astonishment.

"You heard me." Chase bristled, fur standing on end.

"Chill. I'm not challenging you for your woman."

"You're not?" Chase triple blinked. He didn't buy it, but the guy sounded genuine. Nothing made sense—certainly not his own hesitation—and he suspected some sort of mind-magic at play.

"No." Damian shook his head.

"Why've you gone to all this trouble, then? Stalking her. Ransacking her house. Setting her up?" The bastard had tried to murder Arabia and Chase, which really, truly bugged him... except it didn't. At the moment, Chase was cool—as mellow as fine, aged Scotch.

Amid a flurry of flapping wings, a raven dropped out of the sky. Arabia shifted before she hit the ground. Fully clothed, she landed in a crouch, midway between the two men. She placed her hands on her hips and faced the warlock.

"Damian, stop. I won't let you hurt him," Arabia said. Her fierce protectiveness warmed Chase's heart even as he reached to move her behind him.

"Hurt him? Now why would I want to do that?" Damian swung his hands wide, demonstrating his proclaimed harmlessness. No matter how effective the warlock's mystical relaxation spell, Chase hadn't forgotten about those massive silver rings.

"Bastard! You tried to kill us!" Arabia stomped her foot just as Chase closed his hand on her shoulder. He hauled her back and placed her behind him.

Damian scoffed. "That? I was just playing. If I wanted you dead, you'd be dead already. All I want—"

Resentment roiled in Chase's core. Primal instinct regarded Damian as a threat to both himself and his mate. His wolf disliked the warlock and despised the insidious influence the guy exerted over their psyches. A snarl formed in his throat. Releasing Arabia, he advanced a pace.

Damian raised his voice and his fists. "All I want is the return of what is rightfully mine—my stolen property!"

Chase froze midstride. "What?"

"Arabia, tell your lover the truth," Damian challenged. "Why don't you?"

"Now, Chase, I can explain. It's not like he's making it sound."

Chase advanced straight past suspicion to absolute aggravation. He swung around to confront Arabia. He took one glance at her and groaned. She jutted her chin out at a defiant angle, arms crossed over her chest, the poster child for the guilty but newly repentant. It was a look he knew well. *Too well.* Would their daughters be like this? The prospect scared him more than the demented warlock armed with silver brass knuckles.

"Is it true? Did you steal from this man?" Chase asked even though the answer was obvious.

"Yes," Arabia said in a tiny voice. She reached for the braid that dangled beneath her ear and tugged at it. "But it was just a little bauble. I didn't think he'd even notice."

"Not notice!" Damian bellowed. "No one steals from me without me noticing!"

Lightning flashed in the sky and thunder rolled through the clouds, which opened, releasing a sudden deluge of ice-cold sleet that soaked them to the skin within seconds. In unison, Arabia and Chase whirled to face the warlock who was swollen with outrage. Before their eyes, he grew to giant-sized proportions. Golden fire flared about his shifting form. When his transformation was complete, he had the head and wings of an eagle and the body and tail of a lion. He radiated an aura of palpable power.

Griffin.

CHAPTER 20

SHOCK AND AWFUL

The sleet cut at them like a knife blade, but its bite was nothing compared to the chill running through her veins. Arabia subscribed to the basic philosophy of facing one's fears, but this was ridiculous. The full-grown griffin was immense—several times bigger than even an alpha werewolf. Chase couldn't fight Damian alone; it'd be suicide. *If* he had at least a half-dozen packmates with him, they might stand a chance of taking the griffin out.

Maybe.

"Shit," Arabia muttered.

"That about sums it up," Chase said grimly. He caught her arm and shoved her behind him. Again. Still in his wolfman form, he brought up his claws, settling into a fight stance.

The griffin unfurled his wings and dropped into a crouch as though preparing to launch an attack. He glowered, and when he parted his mouth, his roar shook the earth. It was a mystical monster version of shock and awe. The sonic blast hit with physical force. It hurt her ears so much Arabia covered them and took a reflexive step back.

"This is insane." Arabia worked her hands while her mind churned. Obviously, retreat was the best course. She would've fled in a heartbeat except it meant leaving Chase to face the beast alone.

"I'm learning to embrace the insanity," Chase said, tongue in cheek. And, maddeningly, he chuckled low and deep in his chest. That too scared her because she couldn't imagine what he could possibly find amusing in their current circumstances.

"How hard did you hit your head when the car crashed?" Arabia cried out in her unease. She faced a rising tide of panic that made it difficult to think straight.

"Not hard enough." Chase kept moving, leading Damian away from her.

The griffin growled and crouched. He folded his wings and lashed his tail like a whip. The entirety of his attention centered on the werewolf.

Chase snarled and brandished his fangs and claws.

"I want what's rightfully mine." Damian stomped the ground with all four of his huge paws. The thumps traveled through the earth beneath their feet.

"Stay away from my mate. I don't care what she stole. You're not coming near her." Chase's possessive declaration sent a delighted shiver through Arabia. Oh, inappropriate given the present trouble, but she didn't care.

Macho-growly Chase thrilled her.

Damian and Chase circled one another. Mighty roars. Pointy claws. Shiny teeth. Flaunting. Pomp and circumstance. All the male posturing would've been hilarious if only Arabia hadn't been so damn terrified. She was soaked to the skin, and freezing her ass off. A raven couldn't get much unhappier.

"Damn it! This is stupid! Let's talk this through!" Arabia scrambled, trying to catch up with Chase who had led Damian away from her. She tripped over something, though, and wound up on her hands and knees in the mud.

Her mishap triggered mayhem.

Violence erupted. A furious growl erupted from Chase. He drove his claws toward the griffin's throat, seeking to tear it out. Damian shoved his eagle talons against Chase's torso, holding him off. The hooked ends cut deep into Chase's chest, and the rain turned red.

Locked together, the griffin and the werewolf wrestled for supremacy. They traded vicious blows, which left both males covered in bloody gouges. It hurt to see, but Arabia found herself paralyzed, helpless to do anything but watch.

Lightning flashed. Thunder cracked.

Without any warning, the slope beneath the men collapsed into a landslide of muck and churning runoff. The avalanche mired Damian and Chase in its mighty grip and swept them down the mountainside.

Arabia shrieked. Paralysis released her from its hold, so she could act again. She threw up her arms, changed to a raven, and launched herself into the storm.

The wind and hail battered her, but she managed to fight-fly her way downhill. A river of mud flowed down the side of the mountain. Occasional tangles of roots thrust up out of the muck and a few proud, stubborn trees had toughed it out.

About a quarter mile down the slope, the avalanche washed out on a plateau. There, covered from head to toe in brown slime, a griffin and a werewolf formed a tangled heap. A mighty groan issued from one of them, but to which it belonged she had no clue.

Arabia dropped to the ground and shifted to human. "Chase, are you okay?"

The muddy figure she assumed to be Chase lifted his head and asked, "What hit me?"

"Mother Nature. The goddess says you're both dumb asses." Arabia leaned over and caught hold of Chase's foot. She managed to drag him a few inches before he became too heavy. All the while, she lectured. "Damn it! All this violence is pointless and stupid! Chase, he's ten times bigger than you!"

Mired in the root ball of a toppled tree, Damian produced an avian squeal. Arabia didn't speak Eagle but she interpreted the sound to mean, "Shit, that hurts."

She dropped Chase's foot and turned her ire on the griffin. "Damian, you're a cop! You're supposed to be better than this. If the bauble I stole from you is so damn important, why didn't you just ask for it back?"

"It's mine. You shouldn't have taken it in the first place," Damian said, sounding greatly aggrieved.

"I may have some kleptomania tendencies I need to work on," Arabia admitted reluctantly. She grabbed her braid, yanked off the band on the end, and started unraveling. "In my defense, I'm not always even aware when I take things."

"I'm not your therapist. I just want it back." Damian rolled over and heaved to his feet. The filth dampened his natural shiny glow. Feathers on his crest and wings stuck out the wrong way, and his wingtip bent at a painful angle. His tail had the swish of a wet, angry cat. But at least he was talking rather than attacking.

Yay for small victories!

"Hold your horses...I'm working on it."

"My patience is wearing thin..." Damian shook out his wings in a forceful motion that snapped the broken tip into place. Nausea swirled in Arabia's stomach.

"Arabia," Chase muttered. "I'm adding this to the list of things I never thought I'd hear myself say. Give the nice griffin back his bauble."

Both men watched her with impatience and irritation, as though they hadn't been trying to kill each other a few moments ago. Arabia swallowed a snort and a smart remark and worked the braid, fighting her way through willful snarls, which only served to thwart her efforts. It took some painful tugging—and she lost more than a few strands—but at last she yanked the golden bead free.

"Got it! Here." Arabia hurled the hefty bead straight at Damian. She loved the stupid thing, but she never wanted to see it again. It'd brought her nothing but bad luck since she pilfered it.

The griffin raised his claw and snatched the coveted prize from the air. He shot the both of them a final, long glare. "Thank you. I'd say it's been a pleasure, but that would be a lie."

With that, the regal creature flapped his wings and flew off into the storm, leaving the wolf and raven stranded on the side of the mountain. In sullen silence, Chase undertook the arduous climb up the muddy slope. Arabia considered sticking it out with him, but it seemed like he really needed some cooling off time.

She flew back to the crashed car. The sedan smoldered—only a steel skeleton remained. A while later Chase joined her in the woods near the wreckage. And there they stood in the driving rain amid the ruins of felled trees and the broken bodies of hellhounds.

"Whatcha thinking?" Arabia asked in a teeny-tiny voice.

Chase shifted to a man but adopted an immediate expression of regret. She guessed he was as miserable as she. "Fuck," he said, "I need a cigarette."

"No way. If we're getting married, smoking is off limits."

"Yeah? Well, if we're getting married, stealing from griffins is off limits, too."

Arabia offered a sheepish smile. "That sounds fair."

Chase sputtered. "You think those two things are the same?"

"I'm sorry?" Arabia pantomimed a curtsey. She grinned and caught his eyes, trying to coach a smile from him.

"You're sorry?" he asked in a tone rife with disbelief.

She nodded enthusiastically. "I am, and I swear, I'll never steal from a griffin ever again. Though, in my defense, I didn't know he was a griffin."

Chase scowled.

"But that's neither here nor there." She put her hands together and begged. "Will you please forgive me?"

"You think I should forgive you," he said, snapping his fingers, "just like that?"

She swayed, throwing in a seductive shimmy she'd picked up in belly dancing class. "I really do."

"Tempting." War waged on Chase's face. She could see how hard he tried to hold a grudge, and how badly he was losing. He needed another push, and his resistance would topple.

"What if I throw in a blow job?"

"One?" Interest lit his face.

"Ten." Arabia stroked his stomach, exploring rock hard abs. Thanks to Chase being unclothed, all his considerable assets were conveniently, *delightfully* assessable... She liked him like this.

"Done." A groan tore from Chase, and then he dissolved into laughter.

"See, we can make this work."

"C'mere you." Chase swept Arabia up in his arms and crushed her against his chest. He dropped a kiss on her forehead. "I swear, you're gonna be the end of me."

"I love you." She clung to him.

"I love you, too."

EPILOGUE

STEALING HIS BRIDE

February 14th...

The Queen of the Silverwind Conspiracy hoisted the gilt tiara aloft so its myriad jewels sparkled beneath the overhead lighting. Tall and slender, Evelyn Jensen moved with elegance and grace.

Beaming, Evelyn declared, "Now for the crowning touch!"

"Mom, please, this is ridiculous." Arabia ducked, making a half-hearted attempt to evade the headpiece. She raised her hand to fend it off, knowing full well she was doomed to lose in the end. If Arabia resisted too much, her mother had plenty of ravenborn women waiting in the wings to serve as reinforcements.

"Nonsense. You're a princess, and a princess should look like a princess." Evelyn settled the tiara on her daughter's head. "There now, perfect. Doesn't she look lovely?"

Obligingly, the dozen women who made up the bridal attendants oohed and aahed in appreciation. They threw out comments and shameless flattery. The ravenborn women present included Branwen, Arabia's aunts, and various female cousins ranging from first to fifth.

Her twin sister held up a hand mirror, and Arabia checked out her reflection. She fluffed her bangs, and then turned her head to the side. Yeah, she looked good. Her admiring gaze lingered on the gorgeous ruby highlights that streaked her black hair. The expensive beauty consultant had been worth every penny. Going from teal to red had been a good call—a change for the better. Because she wanted to retain part of her old look, however, Arabia had retained her Cleopatra bob.

In keeping with her 1920s style sensibilities, her wedding dress was a modern twist on Flapper fashion. Black and silver sequins in a geo-deco design shimmered like a million diamonds. It had a modest scoop neckline, charming cap sleeves, and a mini skirt fringed in glossy raven feathers.

The outdoor party pavilion bustled with activity as the Silverwind Conspiracy marshaled their defenses with the goal of 'preventing' Arabia's wedding. Six generations of male ravenborn, ranging from Arabia's great-great-grandfather on down to Little Osvifur Harrisson, her fourth cousin who was only two years old, guarded the perimeter. Women and children congregated within the interior, and Arabia and her honor guard sat at the center of it all. As a whole, the conspiracy produced quite the din—festive music and boisterous conversations. Banquet tables laden with food kept the troops nourished, and an open bar kept their spirits bolstered.

"I look like a pretentious peacock!" Arabia complained, again because it was expected of her to play the part of the reluctant bride.

"You're beautiful," Branwen said, offering assurances with a glorious smile.

"Do you think Chase will resent being forced to play along with this silly tradition?" Arabia asked in a low voice, succumbing to the bite of worry. Oh, he'd claimed he didn't mind, but maybe he was only being polite.

"First, it's not a silly tradition." Evelyn frowned. "Second, for a cross-species marriage to work, both partners must respect one another's traditions. I'm sure he's going to subject you to that barbaric biting ceremony to seal the mate bond."

"Mom!" Heat suffused Arabia's face—she was sure she turned beet red. She brought up her hands, begging Evelyn to stop.

"Well, it's true. Don't deny it." Evelyn sniffed. "If Chase Baron wants to marry into this conspiracy, then he will just have to steal his bride like any self-respecting ravenborn male would."

Arabia huffed and raised her voice to carry to the far reaches of the room. "I don't even want to get married to that obnoxious werewolf!"

Evelyn dropped a conspiratorial wink and also shouted, "Don't worry, sweetheart. Your father and brother will protect you!"

An inebriated cheer arose from the menfolk.

"I'm sure." Arabia grinned and nudged her mother. "Mom, tell us about how Dad stole you from your conspiracy."

On cue, the other women chimed in their encouragement, repeated requests for the infamous tale.

"Oh my, your father was so handsome..." Evelyn heaved a dreamy sigh and launched into her exaggerated, fairytale account of her own bridal abduction. The other women listened intently, in part from courtesy, but also because it was a great adventure. Arabia had heard it a thousand times—she knew it by heart—and growing up, it'd been her favorite story.

Surreptitiously, Arabia slid the cell phone she wasn't supposed to have out of her sequined clutch purse. She swiped the screen, opened the chat app, and tapped out a text with her thumb.

Arabia: *Where r u? I'm getting tired of waiting.*

The reply arrived within seconds.

Chase: *Almost there. We ran into some trouble.*

Arabia: *Is the plan to wait until my family is drunk under the tables?*

Chase: *ROFL. Not a bad plan.*

Arabia: *Chase Earl Baron. :-@*

Chase: *OTW*

Arabia put away her phone and rolled her eyes, looking askance at the gods. Overhead, the moon hung full and silvery in the cool, clear February night sky. The gods remained silent, but seconds later, her patience earned its reward.

A great ruckus arose from outside the party pavilion. A wolf loosed a long, low howl that soared through the night. Before it faded, another thirty or forty wolves joined the song.

A howl—Chase had brought the entire pack!

Excitement surged through Arabia. She drew a quick breath and her heart beat in double-time. All around, members of the conspiracy halted what they were doing and tilted their heads to listen.

The wolf pack marched on the gates, still serenading their challenge to a song showdown. Activity erupted everywhere. The ravenborn men on guard duty shouted orders and countermands and dashed to defend the entrance. In less than a minute, they'd organized a discordant chorus. Ravens might not be beautiful singers, but what they lacked in harmony, they made up for in volume.

Arabia cringed and covered her ears. She glanced over at her mother and sister and laughed to see Evelyn and Branwen doing the same. Holding the pose, they defended their eardrums while the vocal war waged between wolves and ravens.

Unlike the majority who faced the gates, Arabia scanned the surrounding pavilion. Her readiness paid off in spades. On the far side of the plaza, Chase climbed over the top of the tall, wrought iron fence and dropped to the patio. A cry of equal parts joy and relief—because the racket was driving her insane —escaped Arabia. She surged to her feet.

Their gazes locked across the distance that separated them. Arabia got one good look at Chase and then grasped her sides and laughed so hard she rocked on her heels. He wore a white fedora, a black zoot suit and red tie, and shiny black and white patent leather dress shoes. Her big bad gangster-wolf —the only thing missing was a Tommy gun.

"Groom at six o'clock!" Evelyn called out. She waved her arm, alerting the rest of the bridal party to his presence.

The other women whirled and hustled to create a living wall between the groom and his bride. Unwilling to miss any part of the spectacle, Arabia hopped onto the chair where she'd been seated. She shielded her eyes.

Chase reached into his suit coat and extracted a velvet satchel. Her fickle bridal party squealed in anticipation. The younger women even clasped their hands and jumped up and down.

"There's no loyalty anymore." Arabia glanced down at her mother, who'd stopped beside her perch.

"Oh, hush. You behaved exactly the same as those girls at your Cousin Gale's wedding," Evelyn shot back.

"The difference being I was twelve at the time." Arabia shut up when Chase reached into the satchel.

Ravenborn tradition required any prospective

groom intent on reaching his fiancée to buy his way past her bridal attendants. His wealth determined the value of the bribe. A poor man could present glass beads, but a rich man paid in gems. No matter what, the offering had to be shiny, or he risked being turned away.

He held a fistful of jewelry aloft for inspection. Gold and silver, emerald green and sapphire blue... it looked like a handsome haul. The bridal attendants squealed and danced, signaling their acceptance. With a grin, Chase tossed a handful of trinkets to both sides and the women dove after them like they'd split a piñata.

Chase took the direct path to Arabia. Evelyn stepped forward and barred his path. He doffed his fedora and dipped in a deep bow. "Your Majesty, may I say, you look stunning this evening?"

"Goodness, who knew you were such a silver-tongued devil?" Evelyn blushed and fanned herself in an exaggerated flirtation.

"The truth can't be denied." Chase winked at Arabia.

Through a heroic effort, Arabia pressed her lips together and kept silent. This moment belonged to her mother. She'd get her turn soon enough.

"An interesting turn of phrase for a man who

wishes entrance into a ravenborn clan," Evelyn observed with a twinkle in her eyes.

"Yes, ma'am." He flashed a wolf's smile, all his pearly whites gleaming, so big and bad...and heart-stoppingly handsome. Arabia felt positive her panties had melted right off and puddled at her feet.

"Do you have something for me, Chase?" Wearing a coy smile, Evelyn crooked her finger at him.

"That I do." Chase fished an expensive-looking jewelry box from an inner pocket. Evelyn moved closer to him, blocking Arabia's view, although she heard the snap when he lifted the lid.

"Oh my!" Evelyn gasped and covered the base of her throat with her hand.

"What is it? Let me see!" Arabia craned her neck and leaned out so far she fell off the chair. She fell... straight into Chase's arms. He scooped her up and cradled her against his powerful chest. She fully expected him to carry her off in triumph, but he didn't.

"Look!" Evelyn held the jewelry box up for inspection. A brilliant diamond choker rested on the crushed black velvet.

Super shiny.

"Oh, wow." Arabia almost swallowed her tongue.

With more than a touch of envy, she eyed her groom. "Did you bring me something, too?"

"You'll just have to wait and see." The man smiled, oh so smug, and Arabia couldn't shake the sneaking suspicion he meant to give her something other than just a necklace. She couldn't wait, so she thumped Chase on the chest, hoping to speed him along. By now any self-respecting ravenborn groom would have his bride over the fence and be miles away.

"Evelyn, do we have your blessing?" Contrary to the core, Chase lingered to make pleasantries. He dropped a placating—and wholly unsatisfactory kiss —on Arabia's brow.

She thumped him again for good measure.

"Oh, yes, of course." Evelyn snickered and shooed him along. "Off with you now. Go make a real woman of my sweet Arabia. This innocent, pure maiden has waited for you all her life."

"MOM!" Arabia shrilled at the top of her lungs. "Pure maiden, my gluteus maximus!" She had more to say but the world spun. Indelicately, she landed on her stomach, slung over Chase's shoulder, staring down at *his* gluteus maximus... and a mighty fine ass it was, indeed.

Chase hustled her off, finally retreating as good

form dictated. Arabia endured being manhandled like a sack of potatoes with good humor. Besides, she had a great view the entire trip. They exited the pavilion through a side entrance, and the second they reached the parking lot, the awful wolf versus raven howl-off ceased. After the bride and groom departed, his family would join hers in celebration. They'd dine and drink and dance through the night.

Chase set her down when they reached his car.

"New ride?" Arabia asked, curiously glancing over the pewter luxury sedan, which still had the dealer stickers on it. Aside from the color, the vehicle was identical to the one that'd been wrecked.

"Yup." He used the electronic key to unlock it and opened the door for her.

"I expected the Porsche." She slid into the plush leather bucket seat and settled in with a smile of pleasure. The interior had that awesome new car smell.

Chase answered only after he got into the driver's side and started the engine. He tilted a sideways glance her way. "I signed the title over to your brother."

"What? Why? You loved that car!" She sat bolt upright, unable to believe her ears.

"Reidar demanded it as your bride price."

"Oh, grr! That jerk!" She fisted her hands and fumed on her lover's behalf. "Oh sweetie, you got conned. He's not allowed to ask for a bride price when you opt for trial by bride-theft."

"I know that."

"Do you? Because Reidar totally cheated you!"

"Arabia, calm down." Chase turned and touched the brim of his fedora, tipping it up. The classy hat bestowed an impossibly dashing aura on him.

"Calm down? But—"

"Calm." Chase silenced her with a kiss. "Down."

Chase's sly smile stopped her outrage cold, and the gleam in his eyes reminded her exactly *who* her brother had swindled: The Alpha of the Baron Pack.

Her husband.

Delighted shivers thrilled through her, and she asked, "Chase, what did you do?"

"Let's just say Reidar's going to get more than he bargained for." Chase chuckled and leaned over to kiss her forehead. "Don't worry, Princess. He won't get anything more than he deserves."

"Chase, when did *you* get so devious?"

"I figured—if you can't beat 'em, join 'em." He grinned and she giggled. Once she started laughing, Arabia couldn't stop even though the infectious humor made little sense.

"Are you gonna let me in on the big secret?" Unable to resist temptation, she grasped the lapel of his jacket and worried it between her fingers.

"Later, important things first."

"What's more important than messing with my brother?"

"This." He took her hand in his own and slid a smooth metal band onto her finger. It might've been tin or platinum. Arabia didn't know or care enough to break eye contact. The wealth of love in his regard was all the treasure she'd ever need. "Arabia Jensen, will you be my lifemate?"

"Forever and always," Arabia pledged with all her heart.

The end.

Tried and true, the Heart's Desire spell is a love charm that requires a deft hand and a pure heart. The witch casting the spell has a mixing mishap, however, and the spell spirals out of control, wreaking havoc through the isolated Sierra Nevada town of Stillwater, California. A storm of sensual shenanigans sweeps up everyone in its path, supernatural and human alike, in a frenzied free-for-all that lasts until dawn. It's more than just hex appeal. It's a recipe for true love when sassy heroines and alpha heroes undergo a trial by love-in to discover their one true mate.

Watch for forthcoming That Old Black Magic titles:

Love is the Law by Melissa Snark

Truth or Dragon by Julia Lake Mills

Branded by Ann Gimpel

The Good Griffin by J.C. McKenzie

Enchanted by Monica La Porta

Beary Sassy by Vonnie Davis

ABOUT THE AUTHOR

Melissa Snark is a paranormal and romance author with a particular interest in werewolves and Norse mythology. Her Loki's Wolves series combines elements of both in a contemporary fantasy setting. She lives in Northern California with her husband, three children and a glaring of cats.

Join Melissa Snark's newsletter to be notified of new releases.

For more information...
www.melissasnark.com
melissasnark@melissasnark.com

Loki's Wolves Universe

Ragnarök: Doom of the Gods Series

Valkyrie's Vengeance (Book #1)

Hunger Moon (Book #2)

Battle Cry (Book #3)

Wolf's Cross (Book #4)

Hunter's Mark (Book #5/Prequel)

Fragile Gods

Blood Brothers (To be released)

Sassafras Shifters

A Cat's Tale (Book #1)

Out Foxed (Book #2)

The Mating Game (Book #3)

Contemporary Romance

Learning to Fly

A Novel of the Fallen Angels

Prophecy

Aries Cursed series

(A Zodiac Shifters Book)

Ram Rugged by Melissa Thomas